Bullets cracked the windshield

Bolan spun the wheel and the vehicle skidded sideways. He heard slugs strike the driver's door, and something burned against his hip, generating a flash of pain. The front wheels hit the soft shoulder, and the SUV lifted as it sped forward. Seconds later it slammed into the massive tree trunk.

The impact hurled Bolan forward, his body twisting, thudding against the door, his head hitting the glass with terrible force.

He didn't hear the other SUV's door slam, or the sound of the engine as the vehicle sped away. At that moment he couldn't hear anything. See anything.

Feel anything….

234.61
258.55

MACK BOLAN ®
The Executioner

The Executioner®
Don Pendleton's

VIRAL SIEGE

A GOLD EAGLE BOOK FROM

W🌐RLDWIDE®

TORONTO • NEW YORK • LONDON
AMSTERDAM • PARIS • SYDNEY • HAMBURG
STOCKHOLM • ATHENS • TOKYO • MILAN
MADRID • WARSAW • BUDAPEST • AUCKLAND

Recycling programs
for this product may
not exist in your area.

First edition September 2013

ISBN-13: 978-0-373-64418-6

Special thanks and acknowledgment to
Mike Linaker for his contribution to this work.

VIRAL SIEGE

Printed in U.S.A.

Whoever knowingly develops, produces, stockpiles, transfers, acquires, retains, or possesses any biological agent, toxin, or delivery system for use as a weapon...shall be fined under this title or imprisoned for life or any term of years, or both.
                              —United States Code 18

Anyone who releases a biological agent on American or foreign soil, with intent to kill, or in any way harm citizens, forfeits any right to leniency. I will hunt down the person, or persons, and I will administer their punishment without mercy.
                              —Mack Bolan

THE
MACK BOLAN
LEGEND

Nothing less than a war could have fashioned the destiny of the man called Mack Bolan. Bolan earned the Executioner title in the jungle hell of Vietnam.

But this soldier also wore another name—Sergeant Mercy. He was so tagged because of the compassion he showed to wounded comrades-in-arms and Vietnamese civilians.

Mack Bolan's second tour of duty ended prematurely when he was given emergency leave to return home and bury his family, victims of the Mob. Then he declared a one-man war against the Mafia.

He confronted the Families head-on from coast to coast, and soon a hope of victory began to appear. But Bolan had broken society's every rule. That same society started gunning for this elusive warrior—to no avail.

So Bolan was offered amnesty to work within the system against terrorism. This time, as an employee of Uncle Sam, Bolan became Colonel John Phoenix. With a command center at Stony Man Farm in Virginia, he and his new allies—Able Team and Phoenix Force—waged relentless war on a new adversary: the KGB.

But when his one true love, April Rose, died at the hands of the Soviet terror machine, Bolan severed all ties with Establishment authority.

Now, after a lengthy lone-wolf struggle and much soul-searching, the Executioner has agreed to enter an "arm's-length" alliance with his government once more, reserving the right to pursue personal missions in his Everlasting War.

Prologue

At some time in the past, the warehouse would have been a hive of activity, with freight being delivered, distributed and driven away. Now the vast building was empty, its only regular visitors rats and other vermin using it for shelter. The wide freight yard's concrete base was cracked, allowing grass and weeds to push through. Empty crates and barrels lay in untidy heaps and the metal chain-link fence sagged, the gates swinging loose on rusted hinges.

Mack Bolan, aka the Executioner, crouched in overgrown shrubbery on the far side of the access road, studying the layout. He had been there for more than half an hour, watching and listening. He had seen a parked SUV tucked away behind a stack of wooden packing crates, but there was no sign of driver or passengers. The warehouse was situated well away from any busy road. The commercial park, long abandoned, was neglected and isolated. It was the ideal place for a clandestine meeting.

Bolan was there to meet a man named Vic Bremner. The soldier's longtime ally and friend Leo Turrin, a former undercover operative who was now deskbound at the Justice Department, had contacted the Executioner with a request for help.

Vic Bremner, himself an undercover FBI agent, had known Turrin for a number of years. A mutual bond had developed because of the nature of the assignments they both had experienced. Turrin's past life as a deep-cover operative embedded within the Mob gave him an understanding of what Bremner was going through, and the younger man respected Turrin's advice and on-the-job experience. Although Bremner hadn't given much background on his current assignment, he did pass on his suspicions that his position was being compromised. Bremner was certain that there was a leak within his department, that he was under threat of being exposed. He didn't know who he could trust within the FBI, so he called Turrin, apprising his friend of his fears. The little Fed knew he had to respond quickly and go to the one man whose integrity was unimpeachable.

Mack Bolan, the Executioner.

Turrin had made contact with Bolan and had laid out the situation. There had been no need for Turrin to plead his case. It was enough for Bolan that his old friend had asked for help.

Bremner had given a location where he could meet with Turrin's contact, and Bolan had acted on it. When his flight touched down at Seattle-Tacoma Airport, the soldier had picked up the vehicle Turrin had booked for him and made the two-hour drive north to rendezvous with Bremner.

Bolan glanced at his watch. Only minutes remained before the meet. He scanned the area, pinpointing the long wooden loading dock where Bremner was supposed to show himself. The difficulty was the black SUV positioned in the freight yard. It told Bolan that others knew the FBI agent was here.

Bolan eased the Beretta 93R from its shoulder rig under his leather jacket. He checked the load and set the selector to 3-round burst.

Vic Bremner had been told help was on the way. Bolan was committed to keeping that promise.

His initial check of the area had shown a gap in the chain-link fence that would allow access to an untidy line of stacked wooden crates. If he could reach the crates unseen, he would have cover that would enable him to get within fifteen feet of the loading dock. After that he would have to reassess the situation.

The soldier glanced at the partially hidden SUV. It was parked in a forward position, so that anyone in the cab would only be able to spot movement through the side mirrors. Less chance of him being seen. The cab's occupants would be watching the warehouse and the loading dock. It was still a risk, but Bolan wasn't about to be offered a better choice.

With his decision made, Bolan broke cover, crouch-walking across the road and through the tall border of grass that had grown up around the base of the fence. He slipped through the gap and settled behind the stacked cover. A space between the crates let him see the parked SUV. No movement. No suggestion his move had been spotted. He made his way along the long tower of wooden boxes until he reached the far end. From there he was closer to the loading dock and the open freight doors.

The silence was disturbed by someone moving along the loading dock. Bolan peered around the edge of his cover. He picked up a man edging along the dock, a weapon grasped in his hands.

The guy on the loading dock paused, turning back and forth. Searching. He carried an FN P90 submachine gun in his hands. Bolan saw him transfer the weapon to his left hand, pulling something from his pocket and raising it to his lips. A comm unit. He was talking to the rest of his team. Whatever else, these people were well organized.

Understanding that only raised Bolan's curiosity. Who were they?

He was supposed to learn that when he met Bremner.

The guy on the loading dock stepped inside the freight doors. He had returned his comm unit to his pocket and was gripping his SMG in both hands as he stepped inside. Bolan saw him glance left and right, in no particular hurry as he moved off the dock.

The man's voice carried to Bolan as he called out.

"Hey, Bremner, show your skinny ass. No more running. We got you pegged, you FBI lowlife."

Bolan decided this was his chance to move in.

The soldier eased around the line of crates, stepping into the clear and raising the Beretta, then ran for the wooden steps that gave access to the loading dock. His feet thumped against the worn planking as he headed for the freight door access, the high, wide gap dark against the exterior brightness.

The guy who had gone inside ahead of Bolan was still on the interior section of the dock. He spotted the tall intruder and swung his SMG into play. Even as he closed his finger over the trigger, the Executioner's 93R cracked, sending a trio of 9 mm slugs into the gunner's head. The guy's skull burst apart in an explosion of flesh and bone. He went down without a sound, his body heaving in a final spasm as he hit the timber dock.

Raised voices from behind Bolan warned him the man's partners were closing in. The soldier dropped prone, anticipating some kind of response. He picked up a shouted instruction, then the twin blasts of SMGs.

Bolan felt the disturbed air as slugs whipped by. He rolled off the loading platform and dropped to the warehouse floor.

The shooters continued to fire, raking the interior in a flurry of autofire. Bolan was safe from the gunfire being on a lower level now. He heard the slugs slamming into objects deeper inside the warehouse. The interior of the building echoed to the crescendo.

"Cover me. I'm out," the guy on Bolan's left yelled.

"Do it fast. I nearly cleared mine," his partner replied.

They were giving out too much information. Bolan acted on it, pushing to his feet. The two shooters were dark silhouettes against the exterior light. As he cleared the edge of the loading dock, the soldier spotted the closer shooter, exposed, his weapon low in his hands as he waited for his partner to reload.

"Son of a bitch," the guy said as Bolan appeared.

He jerked his weapon up.

Bolan's Beretta was already tracked on target. He placed a triburst into the shooter. The guy uttered a strangled cry that was shut off when he took the 9 mm slugs through the throat. He toppled back, in spasm as he went down.

The surviving guy slammed a fresh magazine into his weapon.

Bolan leveled his pistol and triggered a burst that burned bloody holes in his target's jacket. The soldier fired the remaining rounds in his magazine. They slammed into the side of the man's skull, turning him around on one foot before he plunged facedown, legs kicking as his life drained away.

Ejecting the spent magazine, Bolan slid in a fresh one, working the slide to push the first cartridge into the breech. He stood, looking and listening. The warehouse was silent. Tendrils of smoke hung in the air.

"Cooper?"

Bolan turned and saw a figure pressed against the warehouse wall at the far end of the loading dock.

"Bremner?" The man nodded. "Leo sends his regards."

Bremner's relief was obvious.

"Let's get out of here," Bolan said.

Bremner nodded. "Fine by me."

"You armed?"

"Lost my piece when they were coming after me."

"Go pick one up. Those shooters won't be needing them now."

Bremner nodded, turned to move, then stepped back through the open doorway.

The SUV rolled into view, coming directly for the loading bay. Bolan saw a gunman ready to leave the vehicle.

"Bremner. No time. Move."

The guy in the SUV's passenger seat opened fire with his SMG, the random spray of slugs chopping at the timber of the loading dock. Bolan had no choice. He took a dive from the ramp, landing loosely and rolling as the spray of slugs kicked up dirt in his wake. As he went over the edge, he saw Bremner move in the other direction.

Bolan heard the SUV bounce against the edge of the dock. The soldier rolled under the base of the dock as the vehicle slid along the wooden structure. Support beams splintered as the heavy bulk of the SUV kept pushing against them. The vehicle came to a sudden stop. Bolan heard the slap of boots on the main ramp as passengers jumped on.

"Grab the bastard and let's get out of here."

"Get the hell away from me...."

Bolan recognized Bremner's voice followed by the hard sound of him being struck.

"Get him inside. Let's go. Let's move it."

As he crawled along the underside of the dock, Bolan heard the screech of tires as the SUV powered away. He dragged himself out from under the structure and saw the SUV rapidly picking up speed. A rear door swung open, and the upper body of a shooter leaned out, the SMG in his hand angled at Bolan as he left cover.

On one knee Bolan two-fisted the 93R and tracked the shooter. He stroked the trigger twice and saw the shooter jerk, drop his weapon and follow it to the ground. The SUV kept going. It sped through the open gap and careened onto the road.

Bolan raced back to his own vehicle, tossed the Beretta on the passenger seat as he jumped into the driver's seat and fired up the still-warm engine. Dust billowed in Bolan's wake as he powered the vehicle in pursuit of Bremner.

He could see the SUV ahead of him, fishtailing as the driver stomped on the accelerator to increase his lead. Bolan increased his own speed, aware that the narrow back roads that cut through the vast timbered landscape were far from ideal for high-speed pursuits. He didn't let that slow him.

The soldier had come to the freight yard to meet Bremner and offer assistance, and he had allowed the FBI agent to be snatched by the enemy. He should have anticipated such a move.

The tires on his rental car squealed as Bolan threw it around one of the numerous curves in the road. The second he hit the next straight, he jammed his foot down even harder. He was aware that the power of his vehicle's engine was below that powering the bigger SUV. All he could do was keep it in sight for the present.

The area was unknown to Bolan. He had picked up the rental at the airport as soon as he landed and had keyed in the details Bremner had sent to the vehicle's navigation system. That had gotten him to the warehouse. Now he was driving blind.

Heavy drops of rain hit the windshield. It came hard and fast out of a sky suddenly dark with thick cloud, drumming against his vehicle, quickly wetting the road ahead.

The SUV vanished from sight around another sharp bend. Bolan powered up to it and held the rental steady as it slid through the curve.

The green canopy formed by the heavy trees flanking the road shadowed it. Off to the right Bolan saw water gleaming. A broad stream, or river.

He straightened out of the bend and spied the SUV a distance ahead, sitting at an angle across the narrow road. A rear door was open. A shooter faced him, the stubby SMG in his hands clearly visible.

Bolan stomped on the brake, and the vehicle shuddered, its tires burning as they fought to grip the rain-slicked road. He smelled burning rubber.

Then the soldier heard the P90 cut loose. Slugs bounced off the road, then hit the hood of the vehicle as the shooter raised his weapon. The slugs cracked against the windshield. Bolan spun the wheel, and his vehicle skidded sideways. He heard bullets hit his door. Something burned across his left hip, and the soldier felt a flash of pain.

The front wheels hit the soft shoulder and the vehicle lifted as it sped forward. In the scant seconds left to him, Bolan saw the massive trunk of a huge tree looming in front of him. Then his SUV slammed into the wide trunk.

The impact hurled Bolan forward, his body twisting, thudding against the inside of the door. He was unable to stop himself from being slammed into the steel upright of the doorframe, his head impacting with terrible force. He bounced back from it, half-across the passenger seat.

He didn't hear the SUV's door slam. Or the sound of the engine as it sped away. At that moment he could hear nothing.

See nothing.

Feel nothing…

The man had walked out of the darkness, as if the torrential rain had been little more than a slight drizzle. It was one of the hardest rainstorms in months, and it swept down Hardesty's main street, bouncing off the blacktop and drumming against the few vehicles parked against the curb. The man moved slowly, and when he saw the lights of the diner he turned toward the eatery with the directness of a homing missile.

"Will you look at that," Vern Mitchell said. He paused from pouring more coffee into the cup on the counter in front of him. "That feller looks half drowned."

The newcomer paused at the entrance, as if he wasn't certain he should step inside. Then he pushed the door open and entered. The door swung shut behind him, reducing the sound of the storm to a low murmur. He scanned the interior, seeing there were no more than five people in the place.

He looked in the direction of the long counter.

A man was in the act of pouring coffee.

Farther along, and also behind the counter, a young woman stood watching him.

It was Mitchell who broke the silence.

"I'd guess you could use a coffee, son."

He finished filling the mug in front of him, then reached for a fresh one and filled that.

The man crossed to the counter and eased himself onto one of the stools. He left a trail of water across the floor. For a moment he sat staring at the steaming coffee, then reached out to lift the mug.

"Laura, go fetch the man a towel."

The young woman he spoke to turned and vanished behind the serving area.

"Hell of a night," Mitchell said. "You look like you walked a piece."

The man took a deep swallow of the coffee before he spoke.

"Some," he said. Then added, "I think."

His voice was deep. When he raised his head Mitchell saw his eyes were blue, with a startling intensity that kept his attention. The thick head of black hair was plastered against his skull. Mitchell saw an ugly large bruise that started on the guy's upper forehead and ran down the side of his face almost to his cheekbone.

"Some bruise you got. Accident? You have a car accident? That why you're on foot?"

Laura returned with a towel. She handed it to the man and he wiped his face, scrubbed at his thick, wet hair.

"That piece of road north of here can be tricky when it's wet. Since they built the bridge it got kind of sidelined. County doesn't pay it much mind anymore."

That statement came from the man on the next stool. Sam Jarvis was a local man in his late seventies. He had spent most of his life in the town, watching it prosper, then fade when the new highway sucked the life out of it. He knew every inch of the highway in both directions for a lot of miles.

The newcomer drained his mug and placed it back on the counter.

"I'd appreciate some more coffee," he said. He pushed a hand into his pants pocket and pulled out a crumpled fold of notes. He peeled off a ten and placed it on the counter. He watched as his mug was refilled. "Food smells good. What's the cook's special?"

Jarvis grinned. "Whatever she cooks," he said, jerking a

thumb in the direction of the young woman. "That girl is a wonder in the kitchen. That right, Laura?"

The young woman allowed an embarrassed smile to show. "I manage," she said.

The newcomer smiled back. "How about managing me something, then," he said. "Be obliged."

"You like ham and eggs? Side of fried onions and potatoes? Maybe some hot biscuits?"

The man nodded. "Real down-home cooking. That would be fine."

The woman turned and moved into the kitchen area.

"You sound hungry, mister," Sam Jarvis said. "Hope so because that girl cooks something fierce. If she was in a big city, she'd be earning top dollar."

"I'll take your word for it."

"Name's Sam Jarvis," the old man said. He stuck out a bony hand. "I run the local gas station and auto repair shop."

"Matt Cooper."

Mack Bolan took the offered hand, felt the strong grip Jarvis offered. He felt the older man's piercing gaze and knew he was being assessed. He held Jarvis's stare until his hand was released.

"So what happened, Mr. Cooper? You come off the road?"

"Something like that, Mr. Jarvis."

Jarvis smiled. "Hell, only one who calls me *mister* is my bank manager. It's just plain Sam."

"Sam it is, then."

"Now, I'm not trying to drum up business, son, but I do operate a tow truck, and if you need help just say the word."

"Give the man a chance to dry down and eat, Sam," Vern Mitchell said.

"I appreciate the offer, Sam," Bolan said. "But I have no idea where my car is right now."

"It got stole, or something?" Jarvis asked.

"Or something," Bolan said. "It's a long story I wouldn't want to bore you with."

Mitchell laughed. "Hell, son, things get so quiet around here any story would be welcome."

"Ever since they built the bridge across the river and joined it up with the interstate we kind of got shunted aside," Jarvis volunteered. "Town's kind of hanging on by the skin of its teeth. I'm just about ready to hang out the for-sale sign."

"Hell, Sam, don't you get started on that," Mitchell said good-naturedly. "He gets on his favorite subject you'll be here come next Christmas."

Bolan managed a smile despite the bone-numbing tiredness still threatening to drag him down. He couldn't figure out why he was so damn tired.

He pushed his hands through his still-damp hair. He was still trying to make sense of the events of the last… Even that small fact was evading Bolan. Just how long had he been in his current condition?

Bolan drank the rest of the coffee. Maybe the caffeine rush would jolt his memory. He touched the sore spot on the side of his head. He couldn't even recall how he had gained the bruise. Had it been an accident with his car? Or something else? He did know it had affected his memory recall.

Of what?

Where had he been?

Who had he been involved with and why?

He reached his right hand across his body and began to rub the sore spot on his left arm. Above the elbow. It felt like another bruise.

"Son, you look like a man carrying a heavy weight on his shoulders," Jarvis said.

"Some," Bolan said.

Yeah, some, but what?

A young couple in a far booth got up and crossed to the

counter to pay their bill. Then they left, running across to their parked car. It was a lovingly restored 1958 Ford Fairlane 500.

"We still had an American auto industry when they made that," Jarvis said, a trace of regret in his voice.

Bolan watched until the car had turned out of the lot and vanished up the street. A suspicion had flashed across his mind. Then he dismissed it. The young couple couldn't have been involved in his current problem. They were just a couple of kids out for a ride. He excused the suspicion as an aberration brought on by his overwhelming weariness, making him wary in case they were part of the problem.

Whatever the problem was.

He was becoming suspicious of everyone around him.

Yet he felt no doubt in his mind that the people in the diner were nothing but genuine. He couldn't explain the way he felt, just that he trusted them. There did come a point where reality had to stand above paranoia. And Bolan knew that the three people in the diner with him *could* be trusted.

Yet something else nagged at the edges of his reasoning. It had something to do with the safety of these people. The need to protect them.

Again, though, from what?

From him?

That much he understood, though he wasn't sure why.

Was he a danger to them?

Would he harm them?

He denied the thought. There was no way he would put these people in danger.

But maybe you already have, he thought, just by coming here. Walking in through that door could have dragged them into the fire zone.

Bolan turned on the stool to stare out the rain-streaked window. The scene was distorted by the runnels of water. He touched a hand across his eyes as pain swelled in his skull in a rising pulse, dull but intense. It left him unsteady, and he swayed on the edge of the stool.

He needed to go, to get away from this place before he drew trouble to these people. "I have to move on," Bolan said. "I need to go...."

He placed his mug on the counter and slid off the stool, dropping his feet to the floor. But it was suddenly too far down to reach and he just kept sinking.

Bolan wasn't aware he had fallen facedown on the diner's floor, felt no pain when his cheek hit the tile.

Everything closed in around him and he was swallowed by darkness yet again....

2

"Tell me they found Bremner?" Greg Rackham said. "*Please* tell me those cretins managed to locate one man and grab him?"

"Yeah, we got Bremner. He's on his way in now. But some guy showed when we went to pick him up. He took down some of our people."

"If this was a TV movie of the week, I wouldn't believe it," Rackham said. "This guy turns up out of the blue to back up Bremner and makes you people look like monkeys."

"He was better than we thought."

"Is that supposed to make me feel better? We're professionals. Never screwed a contract before. Not good, Nash. Not good at all."

"I feel bad about it myself."

"That's okay, then. You feel bad. It doesn't wash, Nash. If we were still in the service, I'd have had you up on charges."

Rackham listened to the silence over the phone. He had scored a point with Nash, and it made him feel good.

"So say it, Nash. Tell me we're not in the service any longer. Tell me I can't talk to you like that. Go ahead and I'll show you how I feel."

Nash figured now was the time to keep his mouth closed. Bucking Rackham was never a smart thing. The man wielded authority like a weapon, a weapon he could use to great effect. And the man had a point. Nash *had* screwed up. One man made his team look bad.

"So who the hell was he?"

"No clue," Nash said, and even he thought that sounded lame.

"There has to be a reason this guy dealt himself in."

"He must have been another Fed, sent to back up Bremner."

"Did you handle him?"

"I figured Bremner was more important. So we grabbed him and took off. The new guy followed us but we fired on his vehicle and he hit a tree head-on. He had to have been hurt."

"And?"

"We kept going. We should be back in a while. Sooner we get Bremner under lock and key the better. Right?"

Rackham contained himself. "As soon as you drop Bremner off, you get back on the road and find that guy. Do it before he causes any more damage. *Understand?* He could bring all kinds of crap down on us. And send a cleanup crew to move the bodies. Last thing we need is somebody spotting them."

"How did Rackham take it?" Zeke Macchio asked when Rick Nash pocketed his cell phone.

"Not well," Nash said. "He wants that new guy dealt with."

"We still got Bremner here in the car," Macchio protested. "And this rain isn't going to make it easy to track him."

"We deliver Bremner to base, then take off and look for the guy," Nash said. "Or do you want to tell Rackham to go screw himself?"

Macchio shook his head. "No. I'm just a grunt who takes orders."

"That's what I like to hear."

Macchio looked out the SUV's side window. Rain was sweeping in beyond the glass, and the heavy cloud formations were closing in across the area.

"It'll be dark in a couple hours, and it isn't going to be easy tracking in the dark in the middle of a storm. All those trees won't make it any easier."

Nash couldn't argue the point. "Let me have a word with Rackham when we get back. I'll try to talk some sense into him."

From the rear of the vehicle one of the team said, "Hey, good luck with that."

Even Nash managed a thin smile. It wasn't going to be an easy meet. When Greg Rackham turned ugly, reason went out the window. But even he had to see the sense. Nash and his team wouldn't be able to track anyone in the pitch-black and in the middle of a storm. It made tactical sense to wait until first light before they returned to where Bremner's buddy had rammed his car into that damned big tree. If the guy wasn't dead he had to be hurt, and he would have been forced to take shelter once darkness fell.

Strangely Rackham turned out to be in a better mood once he saw Bremner. He listened to what Nash had to say, offering little comment and actually nodding in agreement when Nash suggested a dawn start.

"Just get your team on the road as soon as it's light. Find this bastard. Bring him back so we can question him. We don't have time for problems just now. The deal is too close to completion."

Movement at the far side of Rackham's office caught Nash's attention, and he recognized the tall, black-clad figure of Lise Delaware. She was listening, observing in the silent way she always did. It was unnerving and left Nash with an uneasy feeling.

Her presence disturbed him. Nash was no impressionable novice. He had seen action, had done his share of killing, but there was something about Delaware's manner that made his skin crawl. She very rarely spoke directly to Nash, or any of the men. Her focus was on Rackham. Always Rackham, and the intimacy of that closeness was what creeped him out. He couldn't prove it, but he felt sure there was a sexual connection between the pair.

It was known that Delaware held a high position in the organization. She reported to its leadership and passed their orders back to Rackham. He followed any instructions she gave. Like Nash, Rackham had a military past. He exuded authority, yet he followed the woman's lead without question.

She was scary, Nash accepted, with her slow and deliberate way of moving: the cold gleam in her eyes; the way she flaunted her lithe, sensual body in those clinging black clothes.... She never wore anything but tight black pants and shirts, along with ankle-cut boots, and when she went outside Delaware favored a long, black leather coat. Nash could imagine her devouring her young, and even briefly imagining her and Rackham together unsettled him.

He knew that once he left the office she would express her thoughts to Rackham.

Well, the hell with her, Nash decided. If she thought so highly of herself, she should get out into the field and show them how it should be done. Sitting on her butt, no matter how good it looked, didn't prove a thing. Nash was under no illusions about the woman. She was there to watch over them and report back to the organization. He had no doubts that his monthly assessment wasn't going to earn him very many brownie points.

"I was thinking he might go to Hardesty. It's the closest town in the area. He could be looking for medical attention. Jacobi thinks he might have caught him with a bullet. He put some through the driver's door."

"So get your team in the area. Start from where he totaled his vehicle. Get your crew out there by first light. Do it, Nash."

"What about...?"

"Anyone gets in your way, handle it."

"Do we want to involve civilians? Could bring heavy heat down on us."

"Initiative," Rackham said. "Use it."

BACK IN THE CREW ROOM Nash repeated Rackham's instructions. He added, "Just keep repeating Rackham's name to yourselves. That should do the trick." Nash took a swallow from his glass, his thoughts overlapping as he considered what lay in front of them. "We need to close this mess down before it grows. This is a big operation, guys. If we screw this up, our buddies won't be the only ones dead.

"Go on, get out of here. Get some rest. We move as soon as it's light. Jesus, it's one lousy mother of a mess. We need to bring the guy home alive if possible."

The others wanted to argue the point but they didn't. They did what they were told. No one argued Rackham's orders. The man could be a nightmare. He was Nash's boss, and he made Nash look like a harmless old lady.

Rackham and Nash.

They might have sounded like a comedy duo, but they were a universe away from anything like that. The men were hard bastards who would do anything to protect the organization. They had done, and still did, unspeakable things to protect and strengthen it. In truth they scared the hell out of the rest of the crew. And there was nothing they could do about that. The good thing was they were being paid good money, and that had to count for something.

"Still that same guy?" one of the crew said, picking up the end of Nash's conversation.

"We let him get away. We bring him back or Rackham will slice off our cojones and hang them on a string."

"Him or the black widow?" somebody said.

"Don't joke," Nash warned. "She'd do it and smile at the same time."

THEY MADE THEIR WAY outside as light split the darkness, ignoring the rain, and climbed into the big SUV, Dee Rubio taking the wheel.

"Just get us out of here," Nash said.

"Where to?" Rubio asked.

"Let's pick up from where that asshole crashed his SUV. See where it takes us," Nash suggested.

"The guy was hurt. He had to be," Rubio replied. "His wheels were totaled, so he was on foot. He'd need himself looked at. Maybe he went to Hardesty. It's the only place close."

"Maybe he grabbed some new wheels," someone said from the rear seat, "and took off."

"Then we find out," Nash said. "If there's nothing at the crash site, we start searching. Ask questions. Smack a few heads. Hardesty is a fleabag town off the radar. Think about it. The guy was hurt and on foot. Nothing around him for miles. It stands to reason he might have picked Hardesty because it's all he's got."

3

Bolan was in a bed. That much he figured as soon as he opened his eyes and found himself staring up at a ceiling. There were distant noises coming from beyond the closed door. Voices as well, too subdued for Bolan to make out what was being said.

He checked out the room. Neat. A woman's room going on the decoration and the feminine scents. Bolan recalled the young woman behind the diner's counter.

Her room?

How did he get here?

Then he recalled his fall from the stool. He had been about to leave, to get away from the diner before he brought problems to the people inside.

Bolan sat up, then groaned as a surge of pain lanced through his skull. He braced himself on one arm, touching his head again where the source of the hurt originated. The covers had slipped away, and he saw he was naked to the waist. Down his left side, over his ribs, were angry welts from where he had been thrown against the inside of the door. There was a discolored bruise on his left upper arm. A wide adhesive bandage had been placed over his left hip. He recalled someone asking if he had been in an accident.

Bolan had a vague memory of a vehicle on the road ahead of him. He had been chasing it. They had guns and they were using them. Then he recalled his vehicle being hit. He had lost control…the road wet from the sudden rainstorm…

Was that where he had received the injuries?

He lay back on the scented pillow, staring up at the ceiling again, trying to make sense out of the confusion. But he couldn't. Every time Bolan asked himself a question about what had transpired, he hit a blank wall. Any memories previous to the moment he had walked into the diner had been erased.

As if he hadn't existed beyond that moment.

But that wasn't possible.

He did exist.

His name was Mack Bolan, but using the name Matt Cooper. He had almost given himself away to the people he had met in the diner, had almost given away his real name.

Why the cover name?

Did he need to hide? Was he some kind of criminal on the run from the authorities? He closed down his rambling thoughts and allowed himself to relax. His internal questions were aggravating his headache, increasing the severity of the pain. A faint sound caught his attention. It was the rain being driven against the glass of the window directly across from the foot of the bed. It was still a steady downpour. He watched the rivulets run down the glass while he was in quiet contemplation.

A memory of being out in that rain stirred an image. It came without bidding, and Bolan remembered seeing rain running down the cracked glass of an automobile windshield. He was behind the wheel, staring through the glass and fighting the nausea engulfing him. The pain in his skull was overwhelming because he had slammed his head against the driver's-side doorframe as the car had gone off the road, bouncing across a grass shoulder until it came to a jarring stop as he hit a tree.

Bolan had been driving in pursuit of another vehicle. He remembered that now.

He had been chasing Bremner.

The name came into his mind.

Bremner. Who was Bremner?

Why did he seem important?

He remembered the men with guns.

And they were angry because…because he had shot a couple of them as he had broken out of some building. Then he'd shot another gunner who had taken a shot at him. Bolan felt perspiration bead his forehead. He couldn't recall why he had been chasing the men.

Did they have something to do with Bremner?

He couldn't remember who any of them were, but he did remember having a gun in his hand, which he had dropped in his car when he hit the tree. Shadows on the ceiling and reflections of the rain on the window danced in front of his eyes. Flickering. There and not there, just like his thoughts.

Insubstantial.

Ghostlike.

Refusing to remain still long enough for Bolan to identify them.

And the man called Bremner.

None of it was making any sense. And the harder he tried to bring his thoughts together the further they drifted away.

He felt a rising sense of frustration at not being able to rationalize the strands of thought inside his head. Some inner awareness told him he was a man who normally controlled his own thoughts, knew himself and how he acted in any situation. That awareness now was letting him know he was acting out of character.

The door opened and the young woman he'd seen behind the counter of the diner came into the room.

"Did I sleep all night?" Bolan asked sharply.

The shapely mouth curved in a pleasant smile.

"And a good morning to you," she said.

Bolan realized he had been a little hard. "Sorry," he apologized. "I know that's not the accepted way to say hello."

"You're forgiven," she said lightly.

His first long look at her. He saw a striking woman in her early thirties, with ash-blond hair, cut medium length. From the pronounced cheekbones and the cool blue of the eyes that were checking *him* over, Bolan judged she was of Scandinavian descent. There was a faint, thin scar over her left eye that did nothing to detract from her beauty. Under the light chinos and the short-sleeved blue shirt, the woman's body was thin and supple. "So I have you to thank for the doctoring," Bolan said.

"It's nothing."

"It is to me, so thanks again."

She moved closer to the bed, pointing with her right hand at the adhesive bandage on his hip.

"Why did someone shoot at you? I know a bullet burn when I see one."

"You do?"

"Fourteen months in Afghanistan. Sergeant. Platoon medic." She paused, then said, "And yes, I saw some action. I have bullet wounds worse than yours."

"That tells me a lot."

She cocked her head and regarded him gravely. "You served?"

"A good while back now. And a different kind of action since."

How did I remember that, he asked himself, and nothing else?

She considered his reply, then passed it by.

"It's *Laura?* I heard that in the diner."

"Devon," she said. "Laura Devon. Mom was from a Swedish family way back. Dad's family was originally from Australia by way of England. Both families put down roots in the 1800s."

"Good to meet you, Laura Devon."

The finger pointed again. "You said something about a bang to your head. Looks like it was a hefty one. Is that why you're having the blank spots in your memory?"

Bolan nodded. "I don't remember my past. It's all in there. But I can't get a grip on it."

"Nothing?"

"Just scraps. I know the name I'm using isn't my real one. But I don't know why I use it."

"Maybe you're a lawman, working undercover and using an alias."

Bolan shrugged. "There's a name that keeps jumping around. *Bremner*. Something keeps telling me I've been looking for him. Why? Is he my partner? Someone I'm hunting?"

"From some of the marks on your face and body, it looks as if you've been having a rough time."

He shook his head. There were so many things he didn't have answers for.

"Laura, I'm not avoiding the questions. I just don't have answers."

"In the diner you said we could be in danger. Why?"

"When I crashed I was chasing some people. I can remember that much. There were men with guns. Now they might still be out there looking for me. They could show up here. The last thing I want is to bring trouble to you and the others. Helping me could place you all in the firing line."

"Hardesty might be on the way out, but Sam and Vern are no pushovers."

"Even against guns?"

Devon shrugged. "They won't back away."

"That's what I'm afraid of."

She self-consciously touched the scar over her eye. "I got this when I refused to back off from some Taliban guy who wanted to take away my patient. He had a big knife. I had my issue M9. Guess who won?"

"You. But he got in a close one."

"I came back and took the job here at Vern's because I wanted to work out what else I wanted to do with my life. Hardesty is where I grew up. It's where my folks spent a lot of their lives before they died."

"Both of them?"

"They were in a friend's private plane when it crashed. Happened while I was away." Devon stared out the window. "Never had the chance to say goodbye."

Her story paralleled his own. His family had died while he was thousands of miles away, fighting in a distant war. Different circumstances but the effect was the same. The loss of loved ones through no fault of his own. The pain was just as credible.

There it was again. A flash of old memories.

"Has coming back given you the stretch you wanted?"

"Some."

"And?"

"Right now I'm rescuing lost causes, Mr. Cooper."

"Is that what I am? A lost cause?"

"Not really lost," she said. "Just a little off course."

"I still need to move out," Bolan said.

"You sure?"

"Sitting here isn't going to give me the answers I need."

Bolan threw the covers back and swung his legs out of bed. He felt the room tilt as he stood. He swayed unsteadily until Devon caught his arm and supported him.

"Falling flat on your face again isn't going to help, either, soldier."

Bolan sucked in a breath and concentrated, pulling himself still. He waited until the nausea passed.

"Damn," he muttered. "That knock on my head…"

"Severe concussion can do that to you."

"You think? Standing around in my undershorts isn't going

to get me out there trying to find answers. And where the hell are my clothes?"

"Sit down and I'll go get them. Deal?"

Bolan nodded. He perched on the edge of the bed and watched her leave the room. He admitted he was far from in peak condition. Overnight rest had restored some of his strength, but he needed to gain more. If he could get outside, move around, he might clear away the residue of his weakness.

When Devon came back, his clothes were over one arm. She carried a mug of steaming coffee in the other.

"Try this. Vern is possessive about the restorative qualities of his coffee."

Her words caused a faint ripple in his thoughts.

Someone he knew who had similar views on his coffee. Who, though?

Bolan took a swallow of the hot brew. It tasted good. He had to admit there might be some truth in Vern's claim. He handed the mug back to Devon so he could pull on his pants, shirt and socks. The clothes were freshly washed and dry.

"Did them overnight while you were asleep. Your boots are over by the foot of the bed." She retrieved them for him. "Vern has breakfast on the go." She saw the look in his eyes. "No arguing. Doc's orders. You need food before you go chasing around the countryside."

There was, she had realized, no way to stop him going. Equally her decision to go with him had been finalized, though he didn't know it yet. She would pull rank on him when the time came.

Bolan stood beside the bed, his initial weakness having receded somewhat. He would be the first to admit he was still trying to catch up. He also knew if he didn't move out of here his situation wasn't going to resolve itself.

"Are you too stubborn to let a weak woman help?" Laura asked.

"Never. And *weak* isn't a word I'd use to describe you."

She took his arm and supported him as they walked from the room. He didn't exert himself, taking measured steps until he regained his stride. Even then he let Devon hold on to him. Her firm grip on his arm and the supple press of her body against his was far from unpleasant.

The rich smell of cooking food was just as satisfying when they reached the diner.

"Good to see you around again, son," Mitchell said as they passed the kitchen.

Devon guided him to one of the booths by the diner's main window. A mist of rain drifted across the parking area. Bolan turned and saw Devon cross to refresh the coffee mug she had been holding in her free hand. She poured one for herself and brought them both to the table, taking a seat across from him.

"What's going to happen to Hardesty?" Bolan asked.

"Nothing good," Devon said. "Most folk have moved on already."

"What will you do?"

"That, Matt Cooper, is one of life's unknowns at this present time."

"We'll survive," Mitchell said as he brought over plates of food and set them down. "You kind of passed out last night before you had a chance to eat. Right now all you have to worry about is how you're going to work through my breakfast special before you run off."

Special was the word for the generous portions of bacon, eggs, tomatoes, fried potatoes and beans.

"If I eat all this," Bolan said, "it's a certainty I won't be able to *run* very far."

Devon smiled. "Could be that's the plan."

Bolan caught her eye and saw the faint flush that colored her cheeks.

As they ate Bolan asked Mitchell where Sam Jarvis was.

"He'll be in later. It's early for Sam. Hey, you want me to fetch him?"

Bolan shook his head. "No panic. I just need to ask him about a vehicle."

"No need for that," Devon said. "I have a 4x4 Jeep outside you can borrow."

"I don't want to put you out."

"You won't. It comes with one condition, though. Non-negotiable."

"Go ahead and surprise me." Bolan already had an idea what that condition was.

"I come with it. You're a passenger. With the condition you're in right now, you could fall asleep at the wheel. And I know the area better than you."

Bolan glanced at Mitchell. He gave a slight shrug.

"I know this girl," he said. "She has a stubborn streak I've never seen anyone break. If I was you, son, I'd just accept the inevitable and finish my breakfast."

Bolan might not have totally approved, but he had to agree with the woman's medical assessment.

"You do as I tell you," he said. "No heroics."

"I'll leave that to you. I'm just the driver."

Bolan hoped it was going to stay that way.

4

Mitchell had provided a long waterproof coat for Bolan. Devon was wearing one of her own. They exited the diner and made a dash for the 4x4 parked outside. The Jeep was a few years old but in sound mechanical condition. Devon told him Sam Jarvis looked after it for her and kept it running. The throaty rumble from the engine confirmed that.

"Sam may be getting on, but he's a hell of a mechanic."

Bolan had no argument with that.

"Top mechanic. Great diner. Why would anyone ever need to leave Hardesty?" he asked.

She gave him a studied look. "Are you being flippant, Mr. Cooper? You must be getting better."

"It appears I have a good nurse."

Devon swung the Jeep away from the diner and cruised out of town.

"You came in from this direction," she said. "Let's hope your vehicle is still where you left it."

"When I left, it wasn't in any condition to go anywhere."

Bolan leaned back in his seat. He wasn't feeling in the best physical condition. His body still ached, and the persistent dullness inside his head told him he still had a distance to go in regard to total recall. He had realized his condition stemmed from the severe blow to his head and fatigue following it. A return to normalcy would come only in its own time. Curbing his impatience was a necessity.

"Six miles," Devon announced; she made it sound like a flight attendant telling passengers they had just crossed the Nile River. "That's how far we've come. You had a long walk last night. Especially in your condition. No wonder you fell down."

When Bolan glanced at her he saw the slight grin on her face.

"Are you always this flippant?" he asked.

"Only when I'm trying to cheer up a patient."

They rounded a curve and Bolan spotted the SUV with its nose buried in the thick trunk of a tree. Devon eased her 4x4 to a stop and they checked out the area.

"You were moving fast when you hit that tree. Now we know how you got your lumps."

"Don't remind me."

"So what are we looking for?"

"I'll tell you if I find it," Bolan replied.

He opened his door and climbed out. The rain had washed away any marks on the road. It made him wonder if he had skidded, leaving burn marks, or had simply coasted off the road into the tree. He approached the SUV cautiously, some inner sense telling him to be thorough.

He saw the bullet scores on the hood, door and the windshield; the glass had also been further cracked on impact with the tree. It had been no accident, he realized.

A sliver of recall made him relive the moment when someone had fired at him. His reaction to the volley of rounds had forced him off the road and into the tree....

The driver's door was partway open. He saw bullet holes, which had punched right through the door, and when he checked he saw where a couple of slugs had drilled inside. His hand went to the sore spot on his hip.

Rain had drifted inside the vehicle. The seat leather gleamed wetly. Bolan hunched into his coat as he eased the door wider and checked inside. There was nothing evident until he glanced at the doorframe. The angled metal showed a smear of dark, long dried blood. He automatically touched the gash on his head; he felt a flash of remembrance—nothing more than a fragmentary glimpse in his mind's eye, just like a cinematic jolt from a scene. It came and went in a split second, but it told Bolan this was where he had sustained his head trauma.

Devon was at his side then, holding his arm. She had spotted the blood.

"Was this the place?"

Bolan nodded. "Where I hit my head. Yes. I just saw it. A quick flash. There was someone shooting at me. I was chasing them and swerved off the road and hit the tree."

"Don't try to force anything. Just let things come back naturally."

Bolan stepped away, scanning the area.

"I must have blacked out for a while. Then I remember walking on the road…."

Devon turned him and leaned him against the side of the SUV. She pulled the door wider and checked inside, reaching to open the glove box. She pulled out a folded document. Still leaning inside she unfolded the paper and read.

"The rental form," she said, "is signed by M. Cooper. At least we know where you picked up the vehicle. Seattle-Tacoma Airport. You drove a long distance to get here." She checked out the rest of the vehicle and came up empty. "You either travel light, or somebody has been here and cleaned the vehicle out."

"Most likely the latter."

"I didn't see any cell phone inside. You don't recall carrying one?"

Bolan shook his head. "If I did, I seem to have lost it. I had a gun. A Beretta. That's gone, too."

"Come to think of it, Mr. Cooper, you had no ID in your clothing. No wallet. Nothing except a few dollar bills in a pocket."

Bolan checked the road behind them. "Where had I come from? Where does this road go?"

Devon shrugged. "It runs a long way up country with very little along the route. About three miles back there's an abandoned freight warehouse. It closed down years ago."

She saw the flicker of recall on Bolan's face.

He stared back along the road.

"Something?"

"Can't be sure."

"Give the word, Mr. Cooper, and we'll go take a look."

The rising sound of a car engine broke the quiet. A large SUV burst into view from where it had been sitting concealed from the road. The large tires hit the pavement, squealing as they fought for traction. The vehicle swung off track for a few seconds as it headed directly at them, giving Bolan and Devon time to turn and run.

"Let's go," he yelled.

He grabbed her hand, yanking her close as he dragged her around the front of his wrecked car and into the heavy foliage edging the road. In those few seconds Bolan had realized there was no way they would have been able to outrun the SUV on the road, or even get back to Devon's 4x4 and take off. All they could hope to do was hide in among the trees and undergrowth. It was a thin hope but at that moment they had no other choice.

The solid crack of handgun fire rang out behind them. Bolan heard the sound of the slugs drilling into the surrounding timber. Off target but still too close. Bolan's hope was that their pursuers kept on shooting while on the move; it reduced the chance of them being hit; firing a handgun while running tended to lessen accuracy. He tried to stay in among the heavier stands of timber where the trees were growing closer together. It was the only tactic he had available. He was without a weapon, so he had nothing to fight back with.

Devon moved with him. She made no protest. She simply

matched his speed, gripping his hand with increasing tension. She faltered only once, almost tripping. Bolan held her tightly, practically dragging her back onto her feet. He felt a bullet graze his hip, felt blood trickle down his leg. He ignored the burn and the protest from his bruised ribs. Easing off now would be akin to lying down and quitting. Mack Bolan had no such thought.

They ran for long minutes. The sound of pursuit faded behind them. Bolan maintained their pace. Any gain they might have could easily be lost if they stopped running because they believed their pursuers had quit. He felt exhausted, but he knew they had to continue on. Bolan called on his reserves of strength, hoping he could keep up the pace.

To their right he glanced the silver flash of water through the trees.

"The river," Devon said, gasping for air. "It runs past Hardesty some miles downstream."

"Can we cross it?"

"It's possible, but with all this rain it has probably risen. If we cross it, we hit the main forest area."

Bolan angled her through the trees in the direction of the water.

Devon realized his intention and held back for a few moments.

"Are you serious?"

They broke into the open near the bank. Bolan stared at the swift-moving current.

"It could get us out of this area pretty quickly. If we can get across, they can't follow in the SUV." He glanced at her. "You *can* swim?"

"Well, yeah, but my name isn't Flipper."

"All we need to do is let the current take us. It'll get us away from here."

"You ever sell snake oil, Mr. Cooper, because you talk a good talk."

Bolan shrugged out of the long coat and dropped it at his feet. After a few seconds Laura did the same.

"That's as far as I go," she said. "I don't know you well enough yet to go skinny-dipping."

They eased down the bank and into the river. Almost immediately the current started to tug at them. By the time they were waist-deep, it was taking control.

"Don't fight," Bolan yelled above the rushing water. "Let it take you."

They waded through the deepening water, feeling the current push against them. Overhead clouds, swollen and heavy, closed in. The downpour increased. Hard rain pounded them. Faraway harsh rumbles of thunder sounded.

"We chose a great day to go paddling," Devon said.

"Anyone can do it in the sunshine," Bolan replied.

"So I guess only idiots do it on a day like this."

Bolan gripped her hand tighter as the swirl of water threatened to pull them apart. He hauled the woman in closer until he felt her hip nudge his.

"Why, Mr. Cooper, this is so unexpected," Devon said.

Give me a woman with a sense of humor anytime, Bolan thought.

"Under the circumstances, you'd better call me Matt."

They were in the widest part of the river now. And the deepest. The water surged almost to their armpits. The current had a stronger push, and it was doing its best to take them under its control.

Devon remained silent now. Her free arm gripped Bolan's shirt, her fingers twisting at the material as she turned her body tightly against his. Cold water splashed at their faces as the hard current pounded them. It took most of Bolan's remaining reserves to keep them both on their feet. The riverbed dipped without warning, and even he was unable to stay upright. For a long few seconds they went under, Devon determined not to panic. She would have let go of Bolan if he hadn't wrapped an arm around her and held her tightly.

The rush of water filled his ears. He fought against the current to get his feet back on the riverbed. Once he had them planted, the soldier dug in hard, pushing upright, and felt the slap of rain as his head cleared the surface. Bolan sucked in a breath, then hauled Devon clear. She threw her head back, water gushing from her mouth before she took in fresh air. He caught a glimpse of her face, her eyes wide, her hair plastered to her skull. He had to admire her not going into meltdown. She remained reasonably calm.

Bolan strained against the current. The ceaseless downpour hurled rain into their faces, hard enough to be painful. Foot by slow foot they traversed the watercourse. As they neared the far bank, the power of the current lessened slightly. It was still powerful, but Bolan had his momentum now and he was able to fight against it. He kept moving, not daring to pause. If he did, the rush of water would overpower him and drag the pair of them downstream.

He realized after what seemed a long time that the water was starting to became shallow. It dropped from chest height to his waist. The relentless drag against him slackened. It was still strong but less so. He stumbled over the rocky bottom, into more shallow water, hauling the woman with him.

Knee-high, the rain still falling against them, they dragged their chilled, battered bodies out of the water and collapsed. Bolan allowed them a couple of minutes before he stood, still holding on to Devon's hand. She gave a groan of protest.

"I have an idea," she said. "Let's stay here."

"No quitters on my team," Bolan stated.

"*Oh?* I don't think I want to be on your team anymore."

Bolan pulled her to her feet. "No backing down in midstream."

"We are not in the stream anymore."

"Let's go," Bolan said.

The wooded area protected them from the direct force of the heavy rain but not all of it; water sluiced down through the branches and leaves. The ground underfoot was waterlogged.

They paused by a massive tree and Devon leaned against its thick trunk, shaking her head as she caught her breath.

"I guess I'm not in as good shape as I thought I was."

"You're doing fine," Bolan said.

"We cut through this way," she said. "There's a fire road along here."

As he went to take her arm, Bolan picked up movement ahead of their position. The rainfall had drowned out sound. He pushed her back around the tree, raising a hand to keep her from speaking, then swung around to meet the guy emerging from the thick foliage.

He wore a leather jacket, a dripping ball cap, and he carried a pistol in his right hand, using his left to sweep aside the dripping greenery. His slow gaze centered on Bolan as the Executioner moved to intercept him. The guy's response was fast. The weapon swung around to find its target. Bolan was faster. His left arm intercepted the guy's move, knocking the pistol aside.

The weapon discharged with a loud crack, the slug failing to find a target. In the same instant Bolan's right fist slammed into the gunner's exposed cheek. The guy's head snapped to the side, the cheekbone fracturing from the powerful blow. The guy grunted, momentarily stunned by the force behind Bolan's punch. In that thin window of opportunity Bolan clamped his left hand around the pistol's barrel and twisted brutally. The weapon was wrenched from the man's grip; as he felt it turn, the gunner was too slow to clear the trigger guard and his finger snapped.

Bolan heard the guy's gasp in the moment before he used the heavy pistol as a club to put his adversary down hard. As soon as the man dropped to the ground unconscious, Bolan made a fast search of his pockets. He found a couple of extra magazines in the pockets of his opponent's thick coat. He found a cell phone as well and pocketed that.

"Take this and keep watch," Bolan said, passing the pistol to Devon.

Bolan stripped off the unconscious man's belt and used it to secure his wrists, then dragged him into the cover of thick foliage.

"How did he know where to find us?" Devon asked when Bolan took the pistol back. "Come to think of it, how did they know to come at all?"

He was checking the weapon, a 9 mm Beretta 93F. The fitted magazine was full, less the one bullet the guy had fired.

"It was late yesterday when it happened. Maybe they thought I was dead. Too injured to be any more trouble. It got dark, so they decided to cut their losses until daylight."

"But someone figured to make sure?"

He nodded. "I figure they must be running a sweep along this side of the river in case we made a crossing," he said.

"You think he would have shot us?"

"Maybe. I'm glad we didn't find out."

"Maybe?" Devon shook her head. "Matt, I've decided I don't like your friends."

"Me neither," Bolan said, "and I'm sorry I got you involved."

"Well, I don't think you did that deliberately."

"Nicest thing anyone has said today."

He took her hand and led the way in the direction the woman had indicated.

"You think he might have more friends in the area?"

Bolan understood the meaning behind her question. "He isn't on his own, that's for certain."

"They might have heard the shot?"

"Yeah."

"Then we need to keep moving."

Bolan continued on. Though the narrow path was visible, the foliage and the dense trees pressed in close on either side. He noticed the ground was starting to rise in a gentle slope. He felt the cell phone in his pocket vibrate. Someone was checking on the guy who had carried it. The caller was smart enough not to use a ring tone. That told Bolan that he wasn't up against rank amateurs. The people running the pursuit were astute enough not to advertise their presence more than was needed. Bolan took the cell phone from his pocket and checked the screen.

The screen portrayed a single name.

Rackham.

The name meant nothing to Bolan. He had been hoping it might stir his memory, offer him something he could relate to.

There was nothing else to the text message.

"One of his partners?" Devon asked.

"Yeah, wondering why he's dropped off the grid."

"If we don't keep moving we might be next."

"That's just what I was thinking. Let's go."

5

Bolan let his concern over his lost memories slip away. He needed to concentrate on keeping himself and Laura Devon away from the men hunting them. He had no doubt that the pursuit was still on. If the enemy had come back looking for him after what had happened the day before, it was a sure fact they weren't about to quit now.

With Devon's guidance, they worked their way deeper into the forest, climbing the sloping ground above the river. The woman knew the area well, and she took him in a direction that would keep them clear of Hardesty until they decided on a workable plan.

The forest grew denser around them. The area was almost primeval. They could have been a thousand miles away from anywhere civilized. Despite how he felt physically, Bolan had a sure feel about the forest. There was almost a comfort in being here, deep in the protection of the dense timber and undergrowth. Instincts shadowed by the loss of memory rose to the surface, and Bolan knew this wasn't the first time he had been in similar surroundings. He could react in a place like this, put himself on a level with any enemy. His innate caution clicked into place and he kept himself and the woman moving at a steady pace, his senses alert for any sound, or sight that warned of the enemy.

He had accepted that the men searching for them were just that.

The enemy.

Then he recalled Bremner.

The guy's name slid into place again. This time with clearer remembered images: the abandoned freight warehouse; men with guns and Bolan fighting back.

Images jerking to life like a video being taken off pause. Bolan's meeting with Bremner had been interrupted before the man had been able to brief him. The trauma from his accident had robbed Bolan of the background to this rendezvous with Bremner. He had no idea why he had gone to meet the man. What was behind it all. That, for the immediate moment, was filed away. Bolan and Devon needed to lose their pursuers before anything else could be decided.

The skies opened and the already persistent rain turned into a deluge, sweeping down through the greenery over their heads. The rain hit them like a cold shower, pushed by a wind that accompanied it. Runoffs from the higher ground tumbled like instant streams, sluicing away fallen leaves and small branches.

As they took a break, sheltering against a thick trunk, turning their backs to the heavy rain, Devon pressed close against Bolan.

"We chose a hell of a day for a walk in the woods," she said. "You should have visited in the summer instead."

She felt Bolan stiffen, his hands gripping her and pushing her around the thick tree.

"What...?"

She heard the solid thunk as a slug buried itself in the tree, the sound of a close shot coming with it. As she stumbled to her knees from the force of Bolan's push, she heard more shots, the sound of bullets rapidly leaving an SMG. Flying splinters of wood peppered her back.

"Go," Bolan yelled. *"Find cover."*

The SMG opened up again. Slugs chewed at wood and ripped through the undergrowth, shredding leaves.

Devon threw herself flat, crawling on her stomach, and for fleeting seconds she was back in the Afghan fire zone, surrounded by hostile fire as she struggled to reach a wounded soldier.... She slid across the sodden forest floor, hands sinking into the ground. The heavy rain pounded her.

This, she thought, was crazy.

How could it be happening?

Her hands sank into flowing water and she moved forward into the rushing cascade of a runoff. The water streaming down from the high ground came hard and fast. Before she could pull herself back onto solid ground, the torrent snatched her, dragging her down the slope. Devon felt herself turned and rolled, bounced over uneven ground as the slope became steeper. Water splashed against her face, filled her mouth, and she found herself choking. Gasping for breath, she attempted to pull herself from the runoff. The slope dropped and she went down even faster. With no way to halt her progression she did the only thing she could, using her arms and hands to protect her head.

Her downward rush ended abruptly as she hit the base of the slope, her breath driven from her, water still drenching her. She dragged herself away from the runoff, finding herself on one of the back roads that crisscrossed the forested area.

Devon checked her position, working out where she was, then started along the road, scanning the treelined slope and wondering where Cooper was.

The shots that had echoed behind her made her aware of the position he had been in.

Had Cooper survived?

He had given *her* the chance to get clear, staying behind to cover her.

Was he still alive?

She hated herself for even thinking that way, but she was a realist. Her experience in Afghanistan had taught her a sobering truth. That the good guys could die as easily as the bad. She shook her head.

No.

Cooper had to be alive. In the short time she had known him, she saw the way he faced adversity. He was a fighter. Quitting didn't exist in his universe, and that would be the trait that would see him through a bad situation.

Devon moved at a steady jog, easing her battered body gently forward. She wiped rain from her face and briefly wondered if she would ever be dry again.

Ahead, the road curved to the right. Until she made the bend there was no way of knowing what lay beyond. The sweeping downpour hit the narrow strip of road, creating a soft mist as it bounced from the surface.

When she saw the SUV parked across the narrow road and the armed man positioned against the right front fender, her body tensed. She came to a dead stop, glancing around. There was nowhere to run. Both sides of the road were bound by the overgrown shoulders.

Turn around and go back before he sees you, she thought.

She was out of luck and out of time.

The armed man was already facing in her direction, his SMG swinging around to cover her.

Devon picked up the sound of a harsh laugh above the sound of the falling rain. Glancing over her shoulder, she saw two more gunmen blocking any retreat. A second SUV appeared behind the men, moving slowly as it flanked them.

"Let's go, lady," the man by the SUV said. "Walk to me. Hands where I can see them."

Devon did as she was ordered.

BOLAN LOST EYE CONTACT with Laura as she dropped to the forest floor and crawled away.

He had the shooters to occupy him, and he picked out their shapes through the downpour. One wielded a handgun, the other an SMG. He became aware of the lack of time. The longer Devon was on her own the more likely she might be pursued and captured. Bolan didn't want that to happen but accepted it as a possibility.

The SMG crackled briefly. Slugs hit the tree that provided Bolan with cover. He remained where he was, his low position helping to conceal him from view.

The guy with the handgun used the moment to move forward, semicrouched and starting to circle around Bolan's position.

The Executioner leaned forward, the 93F held two-handed. He caught the advancing figure in his sights and fired, the slug catching the gunner in his side, knocking him off balance. Bolan fired again, his second shot taking the guy in the chest as his body turned in Bolan's direction. He went down and lay still.

The SMG opened up again as the soldier pushed away from the tree, flinging himself flat on the rain-sodden ground. The burst went over his head. With Bolan having dropped out of sight the shooter ran forward, the SMG probing the air ahead of him.

Bolan braced his elbows as he lay on his stomach, the Beretta following the shooter as he advanced. Bolan held fire until he was sure of his target. The Beretta's muzzle angled up as the target grew larger. The guy was peering through the mist of rain, leaning forward slightly as he sought *his* target.

The guy snapped his head around in that last instant, his gaze settling on Bolan's prone figure. It was his last gesture before the soldier hit him with three closely spaced shots from the Beretta. The 9 mm slugs went in through his chest, burning through to his heart. The guy toppled backward, the SMG pointing at the trees' high branches. He lay on his back, kicking, as Bolan pushed to his feet and moved in the direction Devon had taken.

From the high slope he was crossing he could see the narrow ribbon of the road below. It offered little comfort. A road was a conduit that could bring contact with the enemy. But it could also offer salvation.

He kept moving, keeping the fire road on his right at all times. If he lost contact with the road, his survival chances dropped considerably. The vast acreage of the forest could swallow him with little effort. If he disappeared within those square miles of timber and undergrowth, he might easily be lost for good. So keeping the road in sight was a necessity.

The downpour soaked him thoroughly. The ground underfoot, consisting of thick leaf mold, became waterlogged. The soaked leaves clung to his boots, slowing him. Now wind sloughed through the trees, pushing the heavy and cold rain at Bolan, buffeting him.

The driving rain pounded him, flattening his clothes against his body. Bolan found he was fighting for every step.

Below him the narrow road curved away. He paused on the final slope that overlooked it.

Pain swelled again inside his skull, threatening to tear him apart. Bolan slumped back against the slope, fighting the nausea that accompanied the jumbled mass of images spinning inside his skull. He needed to bring his thoughts back on track.

He stayed where he was, rain soaked and hammered by the wind. His gaze was fixed on the road, using it as an anchor point. He ignored everything else, pushed back the barriers blocking his memory.

Bremner.

The name clicked into place again.

He was the guy who had brought Bolan into the game.

He tried to recall the reasons why. How had Bremner made initial contact? Maybe through an association with someone Bolan knew himself.

But who?

The blank wall dropped again, preventing any more clues. It all shut down when Bolan tried to pull other names from the darkness. It ended with Bremner. Anything forward from the man's name Bolan remembered.

The diner.

And the people he had met.

Mitchell and Jarvis.

Devon.

He needed to find her again. It was his responsibility. She had been with him and he had lost her.

Then he heard a raised voice.

Someone shouting.

He roused himself, peered through the greenery to the base of the slope.

He saw movement along the road.

It was Devon.

She was motionless, facing an armed man. The guy was standing beside a parked SUV, his weapon pointing at Laura as he ordered her forward. Under the threat of the weapon, she was complying.

Behind her a second SUV slid into view. It came to a stop. A pair of armed men were already standing ahead of it. A third guy sat behind the wheel.

Bolan edged forward, his own problems forgotten as he took in the scene.

The soldier was in no doubt that the situation might escalate out of control. The opposition wanted him, and he knew they weren't going to be held back by any consideration for Laura Devon's sex.

He scanned the immediate area.

The SUV was parked at an angle on the narrow road.

Devon and her captor were by the vehicle's right front fender.

The two men from the second SUV were spaced out: one near the rear of the vehicle while the third guy was standing by the front door. The driver of the SUV was hanging half-out of the vehicle. Bolan locked onto Laura's captor. He was leaning over her, fingers of his left hand gripping her hair and twisting her head around to face him. He was speaking in a low tone, and Bolan knew he wasn't saying anything pleasant. He knew the situation wasn't likely to remain static. Something was going to explode at any moment, and Devon was liable to be right in the middle.

The young woman was in danger because of her association with Bolan. The fact she knew nothing that could be of help to her captors wouldn't save her from further harm. They had seen Bolan and Devon together, and even though she had no idea where he was the men around her weren't going to believe her. They would hurt her to extract information.

Bolan couldn't let that happen. The woman had put herself in harm's way because she had wanted to help. He couldn't let that backfire on her.

He gripped the pistol, assessed what lay in front of him and made his decision. Whatever was about to go down, Mack Bolan knew he had to stop it.

He pushed upright and powered down the slope, using his left arm to slap aside the wet foliage in his path. By the time his feet hit the trail, he was moving fast. His prime target was the guy hassling Devon. She was too close for Bolan to risk a shot, so he used his momentum and solid bulk to hit the guy. The man slammed into the SUV's fender. He let go of Devon's hair as he collapsed to the ground, the breath driven from his body. Devon slipped to her knees, pulling herself close to the SUV.

Bolan crouched, twisting to meet the closer of his armed opponents as the guy ran forward, swinging his SMG, but hesitating because of the closeness of his buddy. There was no hesitation on the Executioner's part. He had already brought the Beretta into target acquisition, his finger stroking the trigger, sending a single slug angling through the guy's throat. The projectile tore a path up through the guy's head and blew out through the top of his skull.

As the gunner dropped, Bolan saw the guy behind bringing his weapon into play. He fired too early and his slugs went wide. Bolan leaned forward and triggered a shot that clipped the guy's shoulder. The target jerked sideways, using the rear of the SUV as cover. Bolan let the pistol drop and snatched up the FN P90 dropped by the guy he had just put down.

The third gunner had moved around the rear of the vehicle. Bolan lowered himself to the wet road and peered beneath the SUV. He picked up movement as the guy cleared the rear wheel. The soldier thrust the P90 under the chassis and ripped off a long burst of 5.7 mm slugs that chewed the target's ankles to bloody shreds. The man's scream rose above the chatter of the SMG. Unable to stay upright, he slammed to the ground. Bolan laid down a hard burst that took the guy's head apart, his body jerking violently as he was turned over by the force of the blast.

Aware of the second SUV's driver, Bolan rolled beneath the SUV, sliding out the far side, and pushed to his knees. He heard the crunch of the driver's boots on the road and ranged in on the sound. He caught a blurred image of the guy as the man moved across the rear of the SUV. Bolan powered forward in a headlong rush that took him beyond the rear of the SUV, leaving the other man having to alter his position to catch up with Bolan.

The Executioner turned, the SMG locking onto the driver. His finger stroked the trigger and the P90 fired a long burst of slugs that hammered into the guy and kicked him against the rear of the SUV. He hung there for long seconds until gravity took over and he dropped to the ground.

Bolan pushed to his feet and moved around the SUV to check Devon. She was staring at him, her eyes wide.

The guy who had been covering her was struggling to regain his breath, clutching one hand over his body where his side had been crushed against the fender. From the pain showing on his face, Bolan guessed he had broken ribs. Despite his injury, the guy was fumbling to remove a pistol from under his jacket.

The weapon slid free, and the guy began to arc it in Bolan's direction.

The soldier moved in close and used the P90 like a club, swinging it brutally across the guy's head in a left-right arc that put the gunner down on the road. Leaning over, Bolan retrieved the man's pistol and tucked it into his own waistband.

"Promise me one thing," Devon said. "If I ever start to make you mad, just warn me so I can stay out of your reach."

"They weren't about to ask you to join their sewing circle," Bolan said.

"Hey, I wasn't having a dig at you. You just saved my life." Devon managed a smile. "Matt, you just have a way of making a first date unique."

Bolan gathered up all the weapons he could find and dropped them inside the SUV. He opened the front passenger door.

"You want to get out of the rain?"

"I guess. It doesn't seem that I can get any wetter, though."

"Put the heater on," Bolan said as he closed the door.

He could feel the woman watching as he moved from body to body, removing cell phones and wallets. When he had gathered everything he could, he climbed inside and dumped his findings on the floor, dropped the SUV into Drive and headed along the road.

"Where does this take us?" he asked.

Devon didn't reply.

Bolan glanced at her and saw the pale sheen on her skin, the vacant expression in her eyes. He knew she was in shock. Sudden and violent death had come into her life without warning, ugly as only it could be. The woman had been in combat, so sudden, ugly death was something she had seen before. But her experiences had been some time in the past and she had adjusted to civilian life again. The majority of people went through life never having such things thrust in front of their eyes. It wasn't something to be taken lightly. For it to happen again had brought back the dark times she had been through, and it was pulling her into the horror of unexpected violence. Bolan left her alone, giving her space to clear her mind of the images.

He cruised the narrow road. The windshield wipers swept back and forth against the ceaseless rain. Warm air rose from the vents at Bolan's feet. His wet clothes clung to his battered body.

"Just keep driving along this road," Devon said without preamble.

Bolan nodded.

After a couple of minutes she said, "Nice SUV. Top-of-the-line." Then she paused and took a long breath. "Who the hell are these people, Matt? This is still America. Not some Third World country. They can't do this sort of thing, dammit."

Bolan kept driving, letting her work out her frustration.

"But these guys *are* doing it. Right?"

He waited it out, certain what she would say next.

"And it's down to you. There's no easy way to say it, Matt. These guys want *you* and don't give a damn who gets in their way.... Am I right?"

"Yes."

"But you can't figure out *why* they want you?"

"No."

"So what happened before you showed up at the diner?"

"It's what I'm trying to figure out."

"You don't know where you came from before you showed up in town?" Devon asked.

Bolan shook his head. "No."

She made a slight disapproving sound that attracted his attention. "Did I say something wrong?"

"It's not what you're saying. It's how little. Are you always so reticent?"

"All I keep coming back to is that damned name. Bremner. He has something to do with it all."

"Go on," Laura said gently. "Bremner."

Shadowed images taunted him. He didn't force them.

"There were men. Armed. There was a firefight. I traded shots. They wanted Bremner. I tried to protect him, but there were more of them. I couldn't get to him in time. They put him in a car and drove off. I went after them and almost caught up with them. Someone fired on me from the vehicle I was chasing…."

The memory drifted away and his mind went blank again.

"That must have been where you were hurt," Devon said. "The crack on your head. The bruises and the bullet graze."

"Next thing I remember was after the crash."

He banged a fist on the steering wheel. Not being in full control left him frustrated. And not a little angry, because whatever else might have driven him, Mack Bolan was a man who needed to be in control of his own actions.

He knew that much.

Like he knew, for whatever reason, his identity was something he carried beneath the Matt Cooper alias. That his name was Mack Bolan. That he was skilled with weapons and handling himself in dangerous situations. The way he had reacted against the men who had held Laura, placing the young woman in danger. His actions had come instinctively. There had been no hesitation when he was confronted by the hostile attitude of the trio. No holding back. The way he had used the weapons in his hands had been the actions of a man well used to combat situations. His responses had simply happened. He had done what needed to be done.

Bolan considered his situation. The injury from the crash had interfered with his thought processes. But not completely. Slivers of memory had filtered through, allowing him to know his name and retain his physical skills.

Bolan concentrated on his driving. The harder he tried to

pull memories out of the fog in his mind the more they receded. Maybe if he allowed the natural healing process to
develop the easier answers might emerge from the darkness.

The matter was taken out of his hands when a large SUV
appeared in his rearview mirror. It sped up close to the rear
of Bolan's vehicle.

"Matt," Devon yelled.

The enemy had called in additional help.

A second vehicle slithered into view ahead of them, closing in rapidly.

"Where the hell are these people from?" Devon asked.

Bolan was caught between the pair of vehicles. There was
no way to avoid them on the narrow road. No avenue of escape
off road. They had him boxed in this time. It wouldn't have
mattered how much firepower he had. This wasn't a situation
where Bolan could shoot his way clear. And he couldn't risk
Devon being caught up in any further violence.

The soldier braked and brought the SUV to a stop. Armed
men emerged from the two vehicles, covering him from all
sides.

Beside him Devon shook her head. "And *I* asked to come
along."

"Looks like we're going to find out what's going on at
least," Bolan said. "Not the way I wanted, but I guess we'll
get some answers."

6

Lawrence Pembury barely glanced up from checking the figures on his tablet when the door opened and the cuffed figure was pushed into the room. He continued to tap information into the device. It was only when he was satisfied that he glanced up.

"This him?"

One of the armed escorts nodded. "He's not looking so smart now," he said.

Pembury took his first close look at the captive, a tall man, over six feet. He had dark hair and a good physique. The eyes fixed on Pembury were unwavering; a cool ice-blue. There was an extremely heavy bruise on his left temple, a gash in the flesh. It showed deep discoloration. There was a fresh bruise on his jaw. The man's clothing was wrinkled and still bore traces of a recent soaking.

"He give you trouble?"

"He didn't seem to enjoy our invitation, so we had to take appropriate action," the escort commented.

Pembury nodded. That would explain the fresh bruising on the man's jaw.

"Sit him over there." Pembury indicated the chair.

The escorts moved Bolan to the chair and sat him down. While one held his weapon on Bolan, the other secured him with the restraints fitted to the chair.

"Do we have his name?" Pembury asked.

"Are we going on a date?" Bolan asked.

"Spirit. That means he'll resist."

"How about we soften him up a little, Doc. I don't like smart-mouthed guys. Or bastards who kill my buddies."

Pembury glanced at the speaker. "Such aggression, Nash. You should learn to control your emotions."

"That's good advice, Nash," Bolan said. "Maybe you can take a pill to calm yourself down. Ask the doctor."

Pembury stifled a laugh.

Nash stepped forward, his face dark with unsuppressed anger.

"You want to see calm…"

Pembury placed himself between Bolan and the escort.

"You've had your turn," he said. "Now it's mine. You can go."

For a moment it seemed Nash was going to protest. Something held him back, and then he turned abruptly and stalked from the room, his partner close behind. The door closed with a solid thud.

"That man is a thug," Pembury said.

"We can't all be diplomats," Bolan said.

Pembury had crossed the room and was bending over a metal table. When he turned, he had a hypodermic needle in his hand. He depressed the plunger just enough to expel air from the chamber.

"This will help to make you responsive to questions. My employer is going to want some answers from you. For your own sake I would suggest cooperation. I have a plentiful supply of the drug, and he will have no compunction about having me administer more. Believe me, Rackham insists on getting his own way."

Bolan's right sleeve was rolled up. He felt the prick of the needle, then the uncomfortable sensation as it was pushed into his arm. When Pembury depressed the plunger, Bolan felt the warmth flow into his flesh. The sensation expanded.

A comforting glow that spread. Pembury slid the needle out and stood back.

"You can fight all you want," he said pleasantly. "It won't stop it working. I'll give it ten minutes before you'll feel like talking."

He leaned forward to examine the gash in Bolan's scalp. He pushed back the hair, observing the span of the wound. Although the gash had crusted over with dried blood, he could see the extent of the damage.

"Something hit you hard there."

"A car doorframe."

"Did it leave you with a headache?"

Bolan nodded. "An understatement."

He studied Pembury's face as the man peered at the scalp wound again before turning away and crossing the room. He picked up a phone receiver, punching in an internal number.

"I've given him the first shot. Have to wait and see. I've told you it could take time. Fine. I'll do that and wait for you to join us. How long? Give it a half hour."

Bolan watched as Pembury replaced the receiver and walked back to the table where he refilled the syringe. As much as he didn't want another dose of whatever was being pumped into him, Bolan had no say. He tensed his muscles as Pembury brought the thin needle close to his arm.

"If you tense up, all that will happen is the needle breaking off in your arm. That wouldn't be pleasant."

"As opposed to what?"

Pembury slid the needle in just above the site of the first injection. He looked uncomfortable. Something in his manner told Bolan the man was working under some kind of resistance.

"You do this to Bremner?" Bolan asked, watching for Pembury's reaction.

He saw the man flinch. The name wasn't unfamiliar to him.

"Is that why you came here?" Pembury seemed apologetic. "You shouldn't have come."

Bolan remained silent. He had planted the seed. Now he wanted it to grow.

The sensation from the second injection was stronger as the double dose began to take effect. Bolan could feel the warm sensation spreading.

It relaxed him.

It invaded his senses.

It took away any desire to fight the sensation. Bolan drew in deep breaths, trying to resist the warm pleasure rolling over him. He didn't succeed.

He stared at Pembury. The man stood close by, but in Bolan's vision he was a distance away, a distorted image. When he spoke his voice had a hollow, echoing tone to it.

The room shimmered even as Bolan tried to control his vision. It felt as if he was moving, the chair almost drifting. The corners of the room closed in, then parted.

The comforting sensation invaded Bolan's skull, seeped into his brain and rolled his thoughts around. The ache in his head expanded. The pain magnified, and Bolan uttered a low moan as it reached the extreme. White light flared behind his eyes and the intensity blinded him. The spread of warmth from the injections flooded his whole body. If Bolan hadn't been secured to the chair, he would have slid off it.

He experienced an unpleasant floating feeling, a disconnection from his surroundings. His limbs vanished and he drifted… Bolan felt his world implode, and he struggled to keep his eyes open. In the shadows surrounding him, Bolan picked up the low murmur of voices. The voices were too low for him to pick out words.

The disconnection could have lasted for minutes. Or hours. Bolan had no time indicators. No sensation of dark or light.

He tried to focus on what could keep him grounded. Names. People. Places he knew.

He failed. Past and present were slipping away. There were no names to recall. No faces in his mind. All the important markers that determined his existence vanished like water down a plug hole.

Yet he still maintained his hold on his name.

He was Mack Bolan.

So who was Cooper?

Matt Cooper?

Why did he use the name Cooper?

He fought the abyss draining away his memories. Everything he knew. People he knew.

And when they were gone all he had left were the names.

Bolan.

Cooper.

And asked himself the same question again. Who *was* Bolan/Cooper?

The enveloping warmth swamped his body. He fought against it for a while, but it was too strong. He allowed himself to be taken into the cocoon of sensual comfort, drifting away, and it didn't seem important any longer to even consider resisting.

BOLAN CAME OUT OF IT slowly. Even after he had opened his eyes he made no attempt to move. His senses were tangled, uneven, and he wanted to regain some kind of cohesion before he did anything else. After his blurred vision focused in and he was able to check his surroundings, he realized he was no longer in the room where Pembury had injected him. Now he lay on a bed. The ceiling above him was a pale cream with a couple of long fluorescent lights throwing cold, stark illumination across the room. The light pushed into every corner of the room. Nothing was in shadow.

Not even the man seated on a steel chair, the configuration of a shotgun resting across his thighs. When he saw Bolan was awake, the guy stood and crossed to a wall phone. He tapped in a number and spoke briefly. Then he dropped the receiver back on its cradle and crossed to the side of the bed. He was big. Well over the six-foot mark and had the broad-shouldered physique of a dedicated bodybuilder. He wore his dark hair in a buzz cut. He stared down at Bolan.

"Sleeping Beauty awakens," he said. "I was starting to wonder if the doc gave you too much juice and you were dead." He grinned at that. "Rackham would be purely pissed if that happened."

"We wouldn't want to upset Mr. Rackham," Bolan said. He had no idea yet who *Rackham* was; he was having enough problems with his own identity to concern himself with someone called Rackham.

"Rackham is not a guy to piss off."

Bolan decided he didn't care too much for Mr. Rackham.

"Heavy artillery," he said, indicating the shotgun. "That just for me, or are you expecting a war to break out?"

The big guy's brow furrowed. "I never had a chance to use it."

"Well, hell," Bolan said, "that must tick you off."

"It does. What the hell use is a big gun if…?" He paused. "You making fun of me? I could get pissed if I thought you were."

Distracting his jailer had given Bolan the opportunity to check out his condition. The hand restraints were gone, but he had a metal cuff around his left wrist that was attached to a steel cable fixed to a wall bracket.

Bolan considered his situation. His captors wanted him restrained—not dead—that much was a given. So it allowed him some leeway. As long as his life wasn't under an instant threat he had a chance to get away. They wouldn't have gone to so much effort at keeping him alive if they hadn't wanted something from him.

That was the piece missing.

What did they want?

What knowledge did he have that warranted so much effort to extract it from him?

He pushed at the lethargy threatening to shut his mind down. He had already said as much to Pembury why he had come.

It had to be Bremner.

He still had no idea what was behind Bremner's actions.

Unbidden, another name intruded his thoughts.

Devon.

How had he forgotten about her?

She had been with him in the vehicle. They had been together in the forest. Being chased. Then they had been separated and he had gone looking for her. He recalled the confrontation on the road. The men with guns…the shooting. They had almost escaped until being hemmed in by more vehicles. He remembered the drive through the forested countryside, being brought here and Laura being taken away.

Where was she now?

Safe?

She had to be safe.

And where the hell were they?

7

The moment Greg Rackham stepped into the lab he experienced the momentary fear that gripped him each time he entered. Despite the fact the actual laboratory was enclosed in a pressurized room within the room, he still had his moment of discomfort. He managed to keep his fear locked inside. To show it would have destroyed his credibility. Any display of that fear would wipe away the power he had over the facility.

Behind the reinforced glass wall of the lab he could see the research team moving around as they worked. They all wore biohazard suits and full visor-fronted helmets. The helmets were sealed to the bio-suits, and each man carried an independent air-supply unit strapped to his back. They entered and left the lab through an airlock system that jutted from the room. On leaving the lab they stepped into an enclosed section where they underwent an ultraviolet light wash that removed any contamination on their bio-suits. From there they moved through a secondary airlock and stepped into the outer airlock before they removed the bio-suits and stepped out into the main lab. The exit procedure took almost fifteen minutes, but there was no other way the techs could be sure they weren't bringing contamination through to the outside environment.

With the material they were handling, there were no shortcuts. The merest slip in protocol would bring swift and irreversible harm if the virus was allowed to escape. This was a deadly weapon, a silent and invisible killer that struck without mercy and had no boundaries before it became benign after a forty-eight-hour period of activity. During that active period it was a relentless destroyer of life. Airborne, it was easily passed from one host to another. Released in a densely populated area, its potential was unlimited.

In a large city it would strike soundlessly, taking down hundreds, maybe even thousands, and there was no easily available cure. No ready serum. The virus was designed as a weapon against an enemy, and the sole intention was to create sheer panic and a sense of hopelessness because once infected the victims had little chance of recovery.

Rackham watched the activity in the lab. The team was preparing a full batch for their client. The virus would be analyzed by them. The results would be quickly verified, and if the virus checked out as genuine, the client would be coming back for the full batch. Rackham had no doubt as to the success of the trial. The virus had already been tested on live subjects here in the facility. It had worked as expected.

One of the suited workers saw Rackham and raised a hand, extending his thumb as he held up the glass vial in his other hand. It was the sample for the client, ready to be delivered.

Rackham took out his cell phone and keyed in a number. When his call was picked up, he delivered a brief message.

"Tell them it's ready, Lise. Callum will be on his way shortly."

Rackham ended the call and pocketed his cell phone. He left the lab and made his way through to the holding area, where the man named Cooper was being held, and pushed in through the door. Cody stood guard and Pembury was standing beside the bed. He glanced at Rackham.

"He should be ready now," Pembury said.

Bolan saw a well-dressed man pushing his early forties. He looked fit and carried himself like a military man.

Rackham?

He stopped at the foot of the bed, looking Bolan over as if he was sizing up a side of beef.

"So why isn't he babbling every secret in his head?" Rackham said, staring at Pembury.

"I gave up babbling a long time ago," Bolan said.

"You'll find I have little time for levity," Rackham stated. "Don't make things worse for yourself."

Bolan raised his cuffed left arm and pointed across the room at the man with the shotgun.

"It can get worse?"

"I thought this drug was foolproof?" Rackham said.

"He's resisting," Pembury replied.

"Then give him more."

"That could be dangerous. I've already given him two."

"I don't care," Rackham said. "Just do it, Pembury. It's what you're here for. And let me remind you of the cards I'm holding. Cody."

Behind them the shotgunner moved in close. "I'd do what he says, Doc."

Pembury eyed the menacing presence of the weapon. He understood what Rackham was implying. He had to do what the man requested. If he refused, the consequences would be dire. He moved to the bed and raised the hypo he carried. He refused to meet Bolan's steady gaze as he injected the third dose.

The solution circulating through Bolan's system slid him from reality, and he lost all sense of where he was. His view of the room went into soft focus. The people around him ghosted in and out of view. His overriding sensation was of more warmth and a feeling of contentment....

DARKNESS—THEN LIGHT.

Heat and cold.

Mack Bolan felt a combination of sensations enveloping him. He no longer knew where he was. Not that it mattered.

He was unable to move. His limbs and body had taken on a lethargic feeling. He drifted, and then just as swiftly he was back in a hushed reality. No sound. Only a cocoon of silence.

Searing light behind his eyeballs made his head hurt worse than before.

Without warning he began to laugh, a far-off sound that seemed to bounce back to him from the wall of white light around him. He felt the laughter fade, a feeling of anxiety taking its place. His mixed-up emotions swung like a pendulum.

Hot, cold, dark, light, laughter, concern: Bolan fought it all, trying to get a grip on reality before madness took complete control. He concentrated on snatching at a splinter of sanity, holding it in his mind, and fraction by fraction he dragged it closer.

He was stronger than any drug. His will could defeat it. Had to defeat it before the power of the drug scrambled his mind and left him a gibbering wreck.

You are Mack Bolan. Hang on to that.

These people are trying to gain control over your mind. Don't let it happen. Do what you do best.

Fight them.

Survive.

Beat the bastards.

The white light grew stronger, sucking him in even deeper.

Don't let them win.

Keep them out.

You are who you are.

Mack Bolan.

Bolan.

Use the techniques learned at the Farm. What was the Farm...?

SOMEONE WAS SLAPPING his face, rolling his head from side to side with the stinging blows. Bolan opened his eyes and stared up at Rackham. Before the man held his emotions back, Bolan saw something in his eyes. He recognized unease. Rackham was uneasy about something. He was doing his best to conceal his feelings, but in that moment before he composed himself, the man revealed the desperate force driving him. The exposed emotion was gone in seconds, but not before Bolan had registered it. He filed the moment away, hoping his severely disturbed brain pattern would allow him to hold and retain the memory.

"I see you're with us again, Cooper," Rackham said. "Time to start cooperating."

"Cooper?"

"Don't play games. We found your ID in the car you wrecked. Credit cards. Driver's license with your photograph. Matt Cooper. That means I know who you are. More important is *what* you are and what information you carry around in your head."

Bolan let his emotions settle as he stared up at the man.

"It will be in your best interests to talk to me."

"My best interests would be served by getting out of this place," Bolan stated.

"No. Your salvation lies in telling me what I need to know."

"Is that what the good doctor has been pumping into me? Some kind of truth juice? If so, I have to tell you it's been a waste of time because I don't have any idea what you want."

"Cooper, you're in no position to play innocent. Just tell me who sent you here. The same people Bremner works for? Give me what I need to know and it'll all be over very quickly."

"Not much of an incentive for me," Bolan said quietly. "I tell you what you want to hear, then your trained dog over there uses his shotgun to blow my head off."

The shotgunner found that amusing. "Hell, it'll cure your headache for sure."

Bolan turned and looked directly at the guy. He didn't say a word. The telling was all in his cold blue eyes, and the shotgunner got the message.

Bolan saw that Pembury was no longer in the room.

"The medical treatment over?" he asked.

"Pembury went to check on the young lady," Cody said.

"You see, Cooper," Rackham said, "as far as you're concerned this is a no-win scenario. Most definitely a between-a-rock-and-a-hard-place situation. I'm the rock and Cody, over there, is the hard place."

"Dress it up all you want," Bolan said. "I don't have anything useful to say. Between your chase team who brought me here and Pembury's serum, there's nothing in my head. The knock on my head means right now I'd have a hard time telling you what day it is."

"You *know* Bremner."

"The name came to me out of the blue. Apart from that I don't have a clue who he is."

"And you expect me to believe that?"

"Believe the truth. This whole setup is a blank to me. I don't know you. I don't know what your game is. But you seem to know me."

"Your name? That wasn't difficult. Like I said, we picked up your belongings from your car. And you were armed. That tells me you're not just a regular guy. I'd say you were undercover. Just like Bremner. Cooper, I don't like that. It's telling me not to trust a word you say. Which isn't what I need. It's telling me not to turn my back on you. You say you don't know me, but right now you want to tear out my throat."

"What do you expect? As soon as I show up, your trained monkeys do their best to take me down. Haul me and my friend to wherever we are and throw me in here so Dr. Jekyll can pump me full of his drugs. And now you expect me to talk about things I don't have any idea about. And you wonder why I might be a little pissed."

Rackham studied Bolan, his expression changing. He was showing that look in his eyes again, a barely concealed uncertainty the soldier found interesting.

"Things not running the way you expected?" Bolan said. "Screwing with your schedule?"

"Don't push me," Rackham said. "One word and Cody will blow your head off. Just one word."

"If you wanted that we wouldn't be having this conversation. You need me to tell you there's nothing to worry about. There's a reason for that, and until you get the answers you want you have to keep me alive."

"Cooper, you're very sure of yourself," Rackham said. "Don't push me too far."

"The pushing hasn't even started yet."

"Cody, go get Pembury," Rackham ordered. "Now."

Cody turned and left the room, the door clicking shut behind him.

Bolan had been assessing his position even as he kept Rackham talking. Whichever way things went, he figured he had to make a move sooner rather than later. His first priority was getting himself and Laura Devon out of this place, giving himself some space while he tried to work out just what was going on. Confined here, his chances of survival diminished with every passing minute. He was no nearer an explanation but the threat against his life was clear. So he needed to escape.

His first move was freeing himself, getting the shackle off his wrist so he could move freely and at least attempt to break free.

He reached out his right hand and caught hold of Rackham's jacket, pulling the man toward the bed. Rackham's body tilted forward, putting him off balance before he could raise any kind of resistance. He fell across Bolan, who brought his left arm forward and looped the steel cable around his tormentor's neck, pulling it taut. The thin cable bit into Rackham's flesh, restricting his breathing. The man struggled against the coil of chill metal.

"You keep struggling," Bolan said evenly, "and all you'll do is make it worse."

Rackham clawed at the cable. The steel had already sunk into his flesh, and his fingers were unable to gain any kind of grip. He sucked in a ragged breath.

"This won't get you anything," he said, his words coming out in a hoarse croak.

"It appears we're both in trouble, then."

Bolan swung both legs off the bed, fighting the dizziness that swept over him, and maneuvered Rackham around until he had the man in front of him.

"If Cody starts shooting, we'll both get hit," Bolan said. "I suggest you tell him to stand down."

The door opened and Pembury stepped into the room, Cody behind him.

"Close the door," Bolan said, tightening the coil around Rackham's neck.

Pembury moved away from Cody, his eyes flickering back and forth between Bolan and Rackham.

Cody leveled the shotgun, tracking it on Bolan's head. "You let him go," he said.

"Or?"

"Or I put your brains on that wall."

"However close you get, your boss is going to catch the spread pattern. A shotgun isn't for pinpoint shooting. Even you must understand that."

"Maybe I'll still risk it," Cody said, not too convincingly.

Rackham thrust out his hands and waved them at Cody. "The hell you will. For now do what he says."

"He…"

"He's strangling me," Rackham gasped, barely able to get the words out.

Cody maintained his position for a while longer, struggling silently to come up with a workable solution.

Bolan tightened his grip a fraction more, felt Rackham lose a degree of resistance.

"He'll kill him," Pembury said. "The man only has to

tighten that cable a little more and Mr. Rackham loses oxygen to the brain."

Cody wasn't enjoying the fact he had little choice. He was fighting the urge to pull the trigger on Bolan. The barrel of the shotgun wavered. He wanted to fire so bad it hurt, but deep inside his brain common sense fought and won. The shotgun lowered.

"Take the gun and put it on the bed," Bolan said to Pembury. "Fingers away from the trigger."

Pembury handled the shotgun as if it were a live snake ready to strike. He placed it on the bed and stepped away.

"Somebody better have the key for this shackle," Bolan said.

"No chance," Cody said.

"Then I finish Rackham. You pick up your shotgun and take me down and nobody goes home happy."

"Do it." The command rasped from Rackham's throat.

Cody thrust a hand into his pants pocket and came out holding a key.

"Give it to the doc."

Pembury took the key and moved in Bolan's direction.

"You know what to do. Just don't get between me and Cody." Bolan's eyes remained fixed on Cody as Pembury stepped up close. His hand was shaking and he had difficulty locating the key slot.

"No stupid moves," Bolan cautioned the man. "I still have this loop around Rackham's throat."

Pembury finally worked the key into the slot. He turned it and Bolan felt the shackle slip free. Pembury backed away until he was in the far corner of the room. Bolan flexed his left hand as he moved Rackham forward. He maintained his grip on the loop around the man's neck.

Bolan reached for the shotgun, closing his fingers over the weapon.

That was the moment Cody made his move. Taking advantage of Bolan being briefly distracted, he lunged forward, going for the weapon.

Bolan yanked on the steel cable and swung the gasping Rackham aside. The man stumbled, clawing at the cable, desperately sucking air into his starved lungs.

Cody hit the end of the bed, throwing himself across it, reaching for the shotgun.

Bolan had already slid his hand over the weapon. The moment he had a solid grip on the shotgun, the soldier snatched it off the bed. He acknowledged the overwhelming weakness in his body brought on by Pembury's injections and knew he was in no shape for a drawn-out struggle with Cody.

As the big guy reared up off the bed, still clawing for the shotgun, Bolan stepped back. Cody came at him again. The Executioner swung the weapon in a hard, brutal arc that struck Cody in the throat. Choking, he dropped facedown on the bed and Bolan slammed the shotgun down across the back of his muscled neck. He struck hard, and Cody went limp.

Out the corner of his eye Bolan saw Pembury edging for the door. He turned the shotgun in his direction.

"You can forget that, Doc. I need you right here."

Pembury scuttled back into his corner.

On his knees Rackham was wheezing, clutching his bruised throat. Bending over the man and searching him, Bolan located a 9 mm SIG Sauer pistol holstered on the man's hip. He took the weapon and tucked it behind his belt.

Bolan uncoiled the steel cable and pulled it with him. He snapped the shackle around one of Cody's wrists, making sure it was locked. He drew the key from the slot.

Crossing to the door and turning the internal lock, Bolan then leaned against the wall, moving the muzzle of the shotgun to cover Rackham. He turned to Pembury.

"How long will this damned drug stay effective, Doc?"

"You've had three doses. It's going to be hours. A lot will depend on how resistant your system is."

"Okay, now tell me what the hell all this is about. First—who *is* Bremner?"

"He...he was an FBI undercover agent sent to find out what goes on here... Are you going to kill me?"

"I haven't decided yet. Is Bremner dead?"

Pembury's already pasty complexion paled even more.

Before he could say anything Rackham thrust out an accusing hand. "You keep your mouth shut. You know the rules."

He staggered to his feet, still favoring his raw throat. The steel cable had bitten deep, leaving a weeping, livid raw wound on his throat.

"And you, Cooper, are in trouble so deep you'll never get out."

Bolan wedged the shotgun against the man's stomach.

"Take a deep breath and reconsider any threat you're about to make," he said.

"I'd do as he says," Pembury said.

"And I'm going to take advice from you?" Rackham said. "If you'd done your job properly, Cooper wouldn't have been capable of breaking free."

"Now it's my fault," Pembury said. "Every time something goes wrong somebody's to blame, but never Greg Rackham."

"You sniveling..." Rackham said.

"Go to hell," Pembury yelled.

Rackham took a step in Pembury's direction. Bolan hit Rackham with the shotgun, a brutal swing that slammed the barrel alongside Rackham's jaw, snapping the man's head around and dropping him flat on the floor.

"I hope that hurt," Pembury said.

"I think that's a given," Bolan replied. "Change of plan, Doc. We need to get out of here before he's missed." Bolan jerked a thumb at the door. "What can I expect on the other side?"

"The facility. And Rackham's people. There must be a half dozen of them overseeing the research team."

"Researching what?"

"A virus based on the smallpox strain, altered by the techs in the lab."

"You have any idea what Rackham wants it for?"

Pembury nodded. "The man wants to sell it on the open market. It's what this is all about. Rackham already has a potential customer. One of his people is going to make a deal tomorrow."

8

"His name is Ray Callum," Pembury said. "He has a sample vial of the virus Rackham is planning to sell to this North Korean client. It's what they've been working on in the lab the last few weeks. It appears they have succeeded."

"And what the hell is this virus again?"

"A strain of smallpox. Rackham's had the team working on it day and night. I can't give you an insight into how it works because I don't know. All I can say is Rackham had it tested in the lab and made a video for Callum to take along with the sample. It shows the effects on victims he used."

"Was Bremner one of them?"

Pembury nodded. "He is now. Rackham was set on making an example of him. He thought it was funny taking an FBI agent and treating him with the virus. It's his way of showing he can't be messed with. Bremner is badly infected."

"And how did he mess with you?"

Pembury flinched as if he had been physically struck and tears filled his eyes.

"My excuse why I'm doing this? To save my young wife and child. Rackham has her held hostage, and he knows there's nothing I can do because she's an illegal from across the border. My daughter is barely four years old. He has shown me pictures of her and told me what he would do if I didn't cooperate. He's threatened her family, too. Tell me, Cooper, what could I do?"

Bolan could understand the man's dilemma. Whichever way he turned, someone was going to suffer.

"The young woman brought in with me. Where is she?"

"Three doors along."

"Has she been hurt?"

"I don't think so. At least not yet."

"Can you tell me where Callum went? Who he's meeting?"

"A representative from North Korea is all I know. Callum hands over the virus and the video and collects a down payment."

Pembury took a pad from his lab coat and wrote details on it. He tore off the page and thrust it at Bolan.

"This is where Callum is meeting the buyer." Pembury gave Bolan a detailed description of Callum. "They talk in front of me because they have my wife and child. They have me virtually imprisoned here. The bastards are so sure of their power. Sometimes they simply ignore me when I'm in the room. So I stay in the background and listen. I pick up information. Cooper, will you help me?"

"I'll do what I can."

"Then take the woman and get out of here. There are vehicles outside. Give me a couple of minutes and I'll create a diversion. Go and stop Callum from handing over that sample."

"If they find out, it could be hard on you."

"I'll take that chance. The way things are now I'm willing to do anything. I don't expect to come out of this very well, but I have to cling to some kind of hope."

"Would Callum be able to identify me if I show up at this rendezvous?"

"He never comes near this section of the facility. He keeps to his office on the other side. The man is just a negotiator for the organization."

"What organization?"

"The organization behind this operation. I just know it as 'the organization.' Look, Cooper, you need to go now. Before it's too late." Pembury cracked the door and peered into the corridor. "It's clear. Go and get the woman. Wait in the room until I set off the diversion."

"What diversion?"

"You'll know when it happens."

The physician described the route that would lead Bolan to the main exit.

The soldier followed him out of the room, carrying the shotgun, and bolted the door behind him. He followed Pembury to the door the man indicated. Bolts at top and bottom secured it. Pembury left Bolan as he freed the bolts, reaching the far end of the corridor and vanishing around the bend. Bolan eased the door open.

Laura Devon was sitting on the edge of the bed, which was the only piece of furniture in the room. She raised her head.

"Matt! I've been imagining all kinds of things."

"You probably weren't far off the mark."

She went to him and put her arms around him. "What have they been doing to you?"

"I'll fill you in when we get out of this place."

"How are we going to do that?"

Before Bolan could answer, an ear-splitting alarm went off. The high clamor penetrated into the room. Pembury's diversion. He had set off the hazard alarm.

"Come on," Bolan said.

He pulled her behind him, out of the room and along the corridor. Bolan guessed the alarm would be issuing from the lab area, somewhere at the other end of the building.

They were partway along the corridor when a man stepped into view from the intersection ahead. He nodded in Bolan's direction and was moving on when he realized who he was looking at. The guy reached for the rifle slung from his shoulder, his chest heaving as he built up to yell a warning.

Bolan drew down with the shotgun, pulling back on the trigger and hitting the guy in the body. The spreading pattern still had enough kinetic energy to shred flesh and internal organs. The guy flew back, slamming against the wall behind him. He bounced forward, slamming facedown on the floor.

"Let's go," Bolan snapped, the harshness in his tone having the desired effect on his companion.

At the intersection Bolan steered them right, and the short corridor opened into the half-circular entrance area. The main doors were ahead. Moving forward, Bolan pushed open one of the doors, and then he and Devon were outside. It was already full dark, indicating just how long the pair had been inside the facility.

Bolan heard clattering footsteps inside the building. He swung around as an armed man burst through the open door and fired his SMG. The slugs flew into the shrubbery inches away, leaves and branches cascading to the ground.

As the guy prepared to fire again, Bolan triggered the shotgun and hammered the area with a trio of shots. The hail of pellets pounded the target's body, driving him back through the open door. Bolan heard the shotgun click on an empty chamber when he went to fire again. He let the weapon drop to the ground.

The harsh sound of the alarm followed Bolan and Devon as they crossed the parking area. Light from the main building spilled out across the darkness. In the glare of light Bolan saw the rain still slanting down out of the cloudy sky. They were also able to see the half-dozen vehicles parked close by. Bolan chose the closest, one of the big SUVs. He tried the door and found it unlocked. He slid onto the seat and checked that the vehicle was in neutral, put his foot on the brake pedal and pressed the start button. The powerful 3.6-liter V6 engine picked up instantly.

As Devon slid into the passenger seat, Bolan freed the brake, hit the gas and accelerated away from there. He flicked on the headlights, and the twin beams picked out the gap in the weed-choked chain-link fence where the gates had originally been. As he cleared the fence, Bolan saw the narrow strip of road that wound away from the facility and into the dark shroud of the dense forest.

He handed the paper Pembury had given him to Devon. "What does it say?"

"Oh, it's the zip code for a hotel in Seattle. A time and tomorrow's date. Very intriguing but what does it mean?"

"It means we need to get there before a deal goes down put together by a guy named Rackham. If we don't, one of Rackham's men sells a virus sample to a North Korean buyer and negotiates for a larger supply being made right now."

"Are you serious? Is that what all this is about?"

"Rackham has been developing the virus to sell to interested clients. It's a biological weapon a North Korean group wants to get its hands on. The deal is going down at that hotel tomorrow."

"God. Matt, is this for real?"

"As real as it can get."

"What is wrong with these people? They must be sick." She thought about it. "Can you stop this deal?"

"I'm going to try."

"Okay, Matt. Whatever you say."

"We've got until the middle of tomorrow morning."

"We can get to the city in plenty of time."

"Right now I need you to do the driving again. They've been pumping stuff into me and I think it's starting to work."

"What stuff?"

"Some kind of drug that was supposed to make me spill everything I know."

"So everything you're telling me now is genuine?"

"Laura, would I lie to *you?*"

Bolan pulled over, and he and Devon changed seats. She took the wheel and they moved off again.

Bolan leaned back in the leather seat. Now that he had

stopped moving around, Pembury's injections were taking effect.

"Laura, tap that zip code into the GPS and head for the location."

She leaned forward and entered the code. The GPS adjusted the screen image and the quiet tones of the audio guide told them they were on the right road.

"Matt, do you think Rackham will send anyone after us?"

Bolan rolled his head to attempt to clear the fog from his mind.

"Good question," he said. "I haven't any idea. He may be in the dark over the information Pembury gave me and cut his losses. Pembury told me Rackham is working to a deadline on this virus, so that could be his priority."

"Well, that hasn't cleared any doubts I might have had. By the way, are we armed again?"

"One SIG Sauer with a full magazine."

"Matt, you do like to shave the odds in your favor."

His response was slow and quiet. Devon glanced at him and saw he had drifted off into an uneasy sleep.

She hit the headlight full beam, illuminating the narrow forest road, and put her foot down as hard as she dared. She would feel safer once they hit the main highway. There would be more traffic and that would make it less likely they would be spotted.

Or not, she admitted.

She had come to realize the people they were up against were resourceful and violent. If they were still determined to get their hands on Cooper again, they might send someone out to find them.

In her eyes Cooper was one hell of a survivor. He knew how to handle himself, and anything Rackham sent their way would be met with hard resistance. Yet there was no guarantee Cooper could resist forever. He was human after all. A special kind, but still human.

When Devon spotted a diner on the main highway, she coasted into the lot and made her way inside, leaving her companion while she bought a couple of large take-out coffees. She gently woke the man and handed him one of the coffees. She turned the SUV back onto the highway and they picked up their route. She drove one-handed, sipping the hot coffee. Beside her, Cooper stared out through the rain-spattered windshield. He drank, remaining silent, and it was as if she could hear the thoughts tumbling around in his mind. He was trying to remember, the expression on his face telling her he wasn't succeeding.

Devon drove nonstop until fatigue began to have an effect on her, as well. She finally had to give in a few miles from the city and drove into the parking lot of the first roadside motel she saw.

She got them a room, drove to the parking spot in front of it and they went inside. Bolan eyed the bed as if it was a new invention and fell across it, his eyes closing almost immediately.

When Devon gently woke him a little while later, it was to offer him hot coffee and take-out food she had purchased from a store just down the road from the motel.

They wolfed down the food and drank the coffee without exchanging a word. When they were finished, Bolan made for the bathroom, shedding his clothes as he went. He stood under the shower and lathered his aching, battered body until he was satisfied he couldn't improve on his condition any longer. With a towel around his waist he exited the bathroom. Devon had picked up his clothing and folded it. She studied him closely.

"How many times did that man inject you?"

"Two, maybe three times."

"What were they after? State secrets?"

"Rackham was running scared I might have figured what he was up to and wanted to know if I'd passed it on. Me being in partnership with Bremner and all. Or so he thought." Bolan managed a slow smile. "He didn't realize I can barely remember the time of day."

"It didn't stop him trying."

Bolan sat on the edge of the bed as Devon handed him a pack of adhesive bandages. "For your hip," she said. "Now I am going for a shower."

When she emerged from the bathroom, wrapped in a large towel, she saw Bolan had slipped under the covers. She finished drying herself, turned down the lights and climbed into the bed, dropping the towel on the floor. Bolan barely stirred when she pressed against him, and she couldn't hold back a sigh.

Laura, my girl, he is either totally exhausted, or you have entirely lost it, Devon thought.

She decided she preferred the first option.

It was a half hour before the meeting when Laura Devon eased into a parking spot just down the street from the Seattle hotel. While she fed the meter, Bolan sat and checked the area. He saw nothing to arouse his suspicions. He turned his attention to the hotel, which seemed to be fairly quiet, as he would have expected at that time of day.

Bolan stepped out of the SUV. As he made his way toward the hotel, he closed his sport coat over the SIG Sauer tucked behind his belt. They had stopped at a shopping mall on the way in and Devon had used her credit card to purchase the jacket for him.

Devon climbed back into the SUV and sat behind the wheel. She had wanted to go with him, but this time Bolan insisted she wait in the vehicle.

"Hey, you be safe," she said.

"It's my middle name."

She forced a smile. "Oh, sure."

Bolan walked back to the hotel and across the parking

area. He went up to the entrance, the door sliding open automatically.

The wide, open lobby spread out in front of him. The check-in was to his left, staffed by a pair of young women, busy at computer terminals. Directly ahead he saw the tables and chairs fronting the bar area. Muzak played quietly from hidden speakers. Bolan made his way to the bar and caught the attention of the bartender. The bow-tied barman took his order for a fruit juice. The soldier paid and took the drink with him to one of the tables. From his vantage point he was able to observe the two elevators serving the floors.

Now all he could do was wait. Callum wasn't due for another twenty minutes if he was sticking to the schedule Pembury had outlined. Bolan took his time with the juice.

As he watched hotel staff moving around, guests entering and leaving, Bolan allowed his thoughts to meander through the events of the past couple of days. The only fact clear in Bolan's mind was why Callum was coming to the hotel. The man was involved in Rackham's deal. There was no confusion with that.

Pembury's description of Callum made it easy for Bolan to recognize the man as he stepped inside the lobby and made his way across to the check-in desk. Callum was in his early forties, with a stocky physique. He had a thick mustache. In his left hand he carried a medium-size black case that resembled a sample case. The young woman at the desk spoke with him, then picked up a phone and made a call. She passed information to Callum. He nodded and turned toward the elevators on the far side of the lobby.

Callum was showing little sign of being wary. Bolan's escape from the facility didn't appear to have changed the setup. He could only assume Rackham had allowed the deal to go through and hadn't considered Bolan knew about it. That could have been down to Pembury not having revealed what he had told Bolan. It was all guesswork, but the soldier had no other choice. His only option was to keep following Callum and take alternative action if things changed.

Bolan unhurriedly followed the man. Callum stood with a couple of people at one of the elevator doors, waiting for it to arrive. Bolan casually joined the small group, positioning himself behind the man.

When the doors opened five people stepped out. Bolan, standing to the rear of the small group, followed as they stepped into the elevator. He moved to the rear of the car, still behind Callum. The elevator rose to the second floor and Callum edged his way out, Bolan following.

Callum turned left.

Bolan went right.

The corridor Bolan took angled around a corner after a few yards. He took the corner, then flattened against the wall and peered back. Callum was still moving along his section of the corridor. Bolan saw him stop at a door and rap on the panel. The door opened and Callum stepped inside. Bolan retraced his steps, passing the elevator doors, and continued along until he was outside the door that had opened for Callum.

Bolan loosened his jacket around the handgun.

He needed to be inside the room. Logic told him Callum would be passing the contents of his case to whoever was inside. If Pembury's information was correct, that case couldn't be allowed to leave the hotel.

Bolan picked up the subdued murmur of voices from inside the room. Then he sensed one of the voices increasing in volume as someone neared the door. Bolan put his hand on the SIG Sauer. He moved to the side as the door opened and Callum stepped into view—minus the sample case, but now carrying a slim attaché case.

Bolan's left hand flattened against Callum's chest. He pushed the startled man back inside the room, following close. The door swung shut, Bolan pressing against it, his hand producing the SIG Sauer.

"Don't rush off on my account, Callum," Bolan said. "Now back up."

Over Callum's shoulder Bolan saw a slight Asian man looking up from the case that sat on the king-size bed. When he saw the gun in Bolan's hand, he stepped away from the side of the bed, hands half raised.

"Who the hell are you?" Callum said angrily.

"Not room service, that's for sure," Bolan replied.

Callum stiffened, his face flushing with anger. "I thought…"

"Thought you were safe? Sorry to disappoint you, Callum." Bolan saw the rising eyebrows. He took the attaché case from the man and tossed it on the bed. "I know who you are. Looks to me like Rackham isn't so smart after all. Now move over there. Hands on your head where I can see them."

Callum did as he was told, realizing he had no other option. Bolan pressed the muzzle against the side of Callum's head while his left hand patted the man down. He located a solid shape in a pocket. Reaching in, Bolan grabbed and removed a pistol. He slid it behind his belt.

Bolan turned his attention to the other guy. The Asian hadn't moved. His eyes were fixed on Bolan. Not wavering. Simply staring. Assessing.

"Choson'gŭl," Bolan said in North Korean.

The man inclined his head in acknowledgment. "I suspect only a few Americans would know that." Then he allowed a thin smile to show. "Know your enemy?"

"I haven't made up my mind yet," Bolan said. "Open your jacket and toss your gun on the bed, then turn around." The man obeyed. Bolan's visual inspection revealed no other weapon. "Both hands in your pants pockets."

Again the man did as he was told.

"You realize who you are up against?" Callum said.

"If you mean Rackham, I'll take my chances."

"You can't interfere," Callum said. "This is…"

Bolan stepped up to the bed and snapped open the catches

on the attaché case. He raised the lid and saw a three-inch glass vial nestling in the soft sponge protection. It was filled with a slightly milky viscous liquid. Next to it was a slim flash drive; the video evidence of the virus trial.

"For God's sake don't damage it," Callum protested. His voice had cracked, and he was sweating in sheer panic.

Ignoring the pistol in Bolan's hand, he retreated to the farthest corner of the room.

"Not perfume samples, then?" Bolan said. "You want to explain, Callum? Or why doesn't your North Korean buddy."

"Kim Jeung Pak is my name," the Korean said. "And I am not his *buddy*."

Bolan snapped the attaché case shut and moved it off the bed. He placed it on the floor.

"Business associate, I guess. You on your own, Kim Jeung Pak? Or do you have a reserve team in the hotel?"

Pak smiled. "It is not for me to tell," he said. "But if you expect to leave here without problems, then not knowing could make things difficult for you."

Bolan shrugged. "I understand difficult."

"So how do we proceed from here?"

"Listen to me, Kim," Callum said. "This man is out on his own. I believe he was being held at the facility but must have gotten away."

"Remind me to ask Pembury to pump *you* full of something to close your damn mouth," Bolan said.

"Too late. I heard," Kim said. "That leaves you out in the cold."

"Not exactly," Bolan said. "I understand what Rackham is doing. He's working a deal to supply your people with a nasty strain of virus. Something Rackham's people have been working on. I didn't get the full spec, but I can make a guess it's a virulent strain your government wants to use on some unsuspecting target."

"Whatever may be wrong with you," Kim said, staring at

Bolan's facial injuries, "it does not appear to have affected your imagination. Perhaps you should analyze the situation and see where it takes you. Perhaps along a false path."

"Don't try to throw me off," Bolan said. "This meeting was a delivery. From Rackham to you."

Bolan indicated the attaché case on the bed. Kim glanced at the bag and a ghost of a resigned look crossed his face.

"Open it," Bolan said.

Kim did. The case was crammed with banded wads of U.S. currency.

"That takes care of your payday," Bolan said to Callum.

The man wasn't listening. He was gazing at Kim, and his expression revealed the suspicion he was harboring. If Bolan's normally keen insight hadn't been dampened by the lingering effects of Pembury's drugs, he might have picked up on what Kim had been implying himself. Regardless of Bolan's failing, Callum didn't miss the remark.

Perhaps you should analyze the situation and see where it takes you. Perhaps along a false path.

"*Son of a bitch,*" Callum yelled, realization dawning.

He powered away from the wall, his unexpected move catching Bolan off guard. The man caught the Executioner in the side, slamming him off balance. As Bolan went to his knees, Callum recovered and snatched at the handgun Kim had tossed on the bed. He arced the weapon around and centered it on the man. Callum fired, putting a slug into the Korean's chest, knocking him back against the wall. Kim slid a short distance, leaving a smear of blood behind.

Bolan wrenched his own body around, the SIG Sauer lining up on Callum as the man began to turn in his direction. He triggered the 9 mm handgun and put his first shot into the man's right shoulder. Callum gasped as the impact of the slug cracked bone. Still fighting, he tried to realign his weapon. Bolan fired again, this time hitting Callum's lower torso. The force of the shot spun the man off his feet. He thumped to the floor, his body shuddering from the trauma of the shots. The pistol dropped from his hand, and Bolan kicked it out of reach as he gained his feet.

He heard a murmur of sound and looked across to where Kim lay hunched against the wall. He had one hand pressed over the bloody wound in his chest. He was staring directly at Bolan and made a gesture with his free hand.

"Not North Korean," he said as Bolan crouched over him. "South. Undercover. Working with the FBI to flush out a North Korean cell."

"This was a setup?"

The man nodded. He used his free hand to slide a cell phone from his pocket and handed it to Bolan. "Call for assistance," he said. "First number on the call list. Just say Kim needs help. Give them the location."

Bolan keyed in the number and informed the answering voice of the situation, giving the location.

"Your man Kim has been shot. One to the chest. You need to move fast. And bring in the CDC. There could be a lethal virus here. It's secured at the moment, but it needs to be taken care of."

He cut the call and turned back to Kim. The Korean was studying him intently.

"So who are you?"

"A friend. A curious friend. What was this all about?"

"A sting operation intended to catch these guys in the act of buying what's in that case." Kim was losing concentration. His free hand caught hold of Bolan's wrist. "Who are you?" he repeated.

"Not one of the bad guys," Bolan said. "Someone who got dragged into this. Trying to help."

"You with an agency?"

"Only in a loose sense."

"Loose enough to have stepped into the middle of this." Kim's grip on Bolan's wrist slipped away. "Is Callum...?"

Bolan stepped away and checked out Callum. The man was unconscious but still alive.

"Dead he couldn't talk. This way we might get some background from him," he told Kim.

"I hope so."

"Looks like I screwed your assignment."

Kim shrugged. "You weren't to know. Do you have a line on his organization?"

"Some but I need to check it out further."

"You should follow it. Take these bastards out."

Bolan nodded.

The sound of an approaching siren cut the air. Bolan checked out the window and saw an emergency ambulance pulling up outside the hotel.

"What do I call you?" Kim asked.

"Cooper."

"Cooper, get out of here. Members of the Bureau will be showing up any minute. If they find you here, you'll be questioned for days. Go find these people and do what needs to be done. I don't know what agency you work for, but the stuff these people are peddling can't be allowed to be distributed. Find them, Cooper, and shut them down. Permanently."

Bolan pushed to his feet. He put his weapon away.

"You know a guy called Bremner? He's FBI," he said. "They have him."

"It's not a name I'm familiar with. Now get the hell out of here," Kim said again.

Bolan slipped out the door. The corridor was empty. He left the door open and made his way to the elevator, thumbing the button and hearing the soft ping just before the doors slid open. He checked himself out as the elevator descended. No blood on his clothing. He tidied himself up and waited for the car to stop. As he stepped out, he saw white-coated EMTs crowding into the lobby. Guests were milling around in confusion. Bolan blended in with them and let himself be moved along. He waited until the last moment before he reached out and touched an EMT on the shoulder.

"Second floor," Bolan said. "Room 256. I heard shots."

The man stared at him, then relayed the information into the handset he was holding.

Bolan saw the exit in front of him and allowed the press of the crowd to take him through the door. The EMT disappeared in the press of people. Bolan knew the guy would try to alert the police.

He broke from the evacuating crowd and moved swiftly away from the hotel, across the concourse and onto the sidewalk where he slid into the growing crowd of onlookers. He negotiated the sidewalk and made for the parked SUV.

Devon was watching the growing crowd, her face anxious. When she saw him, Bolan caught the relief that showed. He slid onto the passenger seat.

"Let's go," he said. "But do it calmly. No screeching tires and burning rubber."

"As if," she said.

She pulled away with remarkable restraint, despite the rising sound of police sirens. As she slid into traffic, a couple of police cruisers whipped by, sirens at full pitch and lights flashing.

"Where to?"

"Right now anywhere away from the area. When the police find the vial of virus in that room, this part of town will be sealed tight."

She glanced at him. "So what happened?"

"The North Korean buyer turned out to be an undercover agent."

"If that had come from anyone else, Matt, I would have thought it was a bad joke."

"No joke," Bolan said.

"So how did it end?"

"Callum wounded the agent."

"And you shot Callum," Devon said. "How did I know that?"

Bolan showed a weary smile. "It's a gift you have."

"Is Callum dead?"

"No. The FBI will be able to talk to him."

"There's a blessing," Devon said.

"Cynical, aren't we?"

She smiled. "Must be the effect of hanging out with you."

"That's over," Bolan said. "Laura, I can't let you stay with me any longer. This is getting out of hand."

"I know what I'm letting myself in for."

"So do I," Bolan said. "That's why I want you out of harm's way. I need to go back to the facility and shut this operation down before Rackham takes it up a notch. You've helped me, but it's time for you to walk away. I need to focus on what I'm doing. If I have you alongside, it means taking my eye off the ball. No offense, but I can't have you there." Bolan saw the look in her eyes. "Don't hold it against me. I can't chance having anything happen to you."

Devon concealed her disappointment, but she admitted he was right. If he was going up against Rackham, he needed to be able to concentrate fully on that. Not be concerned that she was shadowing him and hanging that responsibility around his neck.

"Then I'll drive to where I left my vehicle and I'll go back to the diner." Bolan nodded. She glanced at him. "You're not going to drive up to the gate and ask to be let back in, are you?"

"I think I can be a little more subtle than that."

"Oh? So what will you do?"

"Go in on foot. No warning. Catch them off guard."

"Sounds good on paper," she said.

"My instinct tells me I've done this before, so I'll work on that basis."

THE TRIP BACK ALLOWED Bolan to rest again, trying to shake off the lingering effects of Pembury's drugs. He had no other means of recuperating open to him. And knowing what lay ahead he couldn't afford to delay his return. When news of what had happened at the hotel reached Rackham, he was going to push to complete the full batch of the virus and make alternative arrangements with his buyer.

Watching the forested landscape flash by, the heavy clouded sky threatening more rain, Bolan stirred restlessly. His mind was churning with half-remembered images. Faces. Places. Always just out of reach. Ready to slip away the moment he tried to focus on them.

He glanced at Devon, her face in profile as she drove. Right at that moment she seemed the only real thing in his life. Since he had met her, she had been solid and dependable, with him through the hectic moments, and never once complaining. He would miss her. But rather that than have anything happen to her.

"MY CAR IS ABOUT TWO MILES away."

"You go straight to the diner," Bolan said. "No diversions."

"Are you sure about this?" Devon asked.

"No discussion, Laura. Rackham is going to be ready to tear out my throat. No way I want you near that place."

Devon eased off the gas and coasted to a stop, scanning the area. She sat for a while, searching the way ahead.

"I can make it from here. Trust me. I know the area. I can cut through the trees and check it out before I go for it. Like you said, Matt, I'm a liability. Let me go now."

Bolan reached out and touched her cheek. "You are a hell of a soldier, Laura Devon. Good to have known you."

He leaned and kissed her gently on the lips.

Devon cleared her throat. "Turn around. Stay on this road for six miles. You'll hit a steep climb. Just follow it. The facility is around fifteen miles farther on. When the pavement ends and it's dirt you'll be close."

"You remembered that?"

She nodded. "Not a route I'm likely to forget. Now get moving, mister. And you better come calling when this is over."

She slipped out the passenger door, closed it, then crossed into the thick undergrowth, quickly vanishing in the dense clusters of trees.

Bolan swung the SUV around and stepped on the gas.

He set his mind on what lay ahead, trying to put Devon out of his thoughts. He smiled at that. Here he was trying to recall past memories and now he was deliberately trying to lose one.

9

Rick Nash and Zeke Macchio sat in their SUV on the approach to Hardesty simply watching. Nash's instincts told him this was the place to be. While the rest of Rackham's people were searching the forest around the facility, Nash had driven the route that ended at Hardesty.

"I think the woman will come home," Nash said. "Cooper will drop her off and head out. She'll come back to Hardesty."

"You know she's from Hardesty?" Macchio said. "How?"

Nash tapped the side of his head. "While Rackham was making noises and giving the rest of the guys a hard time, I used my brain. I contacted base and had them run a check on the vehicle the woman and Cooper were in when they were taken, a 4x4 Jeep. It's registered to her…Laura Devon. Hometown is Hardesty. Background check showed she was in the military. Medic in Afghanistan. Just the person to patch Cooper up."

"Regular Girl Scout," Macchio said. "You tell Rackham all this?"

Nash smiled. "Later maybe. He's got enough to handle with the deal going south."

"Nothing to do with you coming up looking good?"

"Shame on you, Zeke. Would I pull something like that on our beloved boss?"

"Oh, yes," Macchio said. "Not to mention impressing the bitch from hell."

"Can't say I like her much, but she has clout with the top dogs. So it doesn't hurt to keep in her good books."

Macchio stared out through the windshield, working out things in his mind.

"So you figure the woman will lead us to Cooper?"

"Maybe. If the guy's still alive. He was banged up when he totaled his vehicle. He took a hell of a whack on his head. Pembury pumped him full of that serum to loosen his tongue because Rackham wanted to find out how much he knew about Bremner. Then there was the screwup with the virus."

THERE HAD BEEN NO SIGN of Cooper and the woman since they had broken out of the facility until Cooper had shown up at the hotel where Callum was to pass along the virus sample.

Rackham had a spotter team on the street in case Callum needed protection. They were too late. The only solid piece of information they got was a sighting of Cooper leaving the hotel and getting into the SUV he had commandeered on his escape from the facility. They were unable to follow him due to the snarl of traffic outside the hotel as every police cruiser showed up to control the crowd. By the time they broke through and took the road out of town, Cooper was long gone. Calling Rackham only earned the spotter team a wild tirade. It was obvious the deal had been blown apart, and the matter was further confirmed by the arrival of both the FBI and a vehicle from the CDC at the hotel. Rackham's team had seen Callum being taken away by ambulance, one of the FBI vehicles following. A second ambulance ferried an Asian man out of the area shortly after.

Rackham ordered his people back to the facility while he rapidly altered his plans. He had contacted the North Koreans, explained what had happened and promised them a fresh virus sample. He had realized the security of the facility might have been compromised and made the decision to move their handover of the sample to a fresh location. With the Koreans reasonably mollified, Rackham had marshaled his remaining team into search mode. He was aware that his principals wouldn't be happy over the breaches in security, and he needed to show he was still in control.

Cooper was still a threat. As long as he was out there he had the power to cause more problems. Rackham wanted him back. He needed to find out Cooper's background and what information he had on the organization. It was important to Rackham that he still had the approval of the top echelon.

He sent out the teams. Searching for and finding Cooper was their objective. Rackham made that clear.

Nash had quietly indicated for Macchio to stay close as they exited the facility and climbed into their SUV. Nash had waited until the rest of the team had dispersed before driving out of the compound. He had taken the route away from the general search area.

"Where are we going?" Macchio asked.

"Patience," Nash said.

"You working one of your hunches?"

Nash grinned. "I don't care what they say about you, Zeke—you're a sharp guy."

Macchio wasn't convinced that was a compliment.

NASH HAD DRIVEN OFF the road, concealing the SUV in the thick undergrowth and trees that bordered it.

"What if Cooper *doesn't* drop the woman off?" Macchio said. "Maybe he'll keep her with him."

"Uh-uh. This time he's going to be on his own. He'll want the girl out of harm's way. He had no choice when we grabbed him last time. Cooper is the kind of guy who won't put her back at risk if he has any say in it."

"So why are *we* wasting time here?"

"Leverage," Nash said. "We take charge of the woman. Haul her back to the base."

"We put her back on the firing line?"

"Simple," Nash said.

"If it's that simple," Macchio said, "why didn't we wait and take them both?"

"Because we would have ended up in a firefight. We could have been hurt, Cooper could have ended up dead, and Rackham wouldn't have been pleased if all we had to show was a dead body. This way we snatch the woman and take her back. Gives *us* an advantage. Cooper for the woman."

"Sounds good. But Rackham isn't going to be happy having a witness walk away."

"The woman? When Cooper comes after her we have them both. Rackham won't let her walk free once she's been used."

"That is a sneaky plan, Nash."

"Isn't it just," Nash said. "Think of it as gaining a tactical advantage. Cooper is less likely to go hog wild if the woman is around."

"We've got to get to her first," Macchio pointed out.

Nash had been scanning the open road, using binoculars, following the curve that allowed him to see what was approaching from a good distance away.

"Keep the faith," he said.

"When Rackham finds out we've been sitting here instead of looking for Cooper, we'll need more than faith on our side."

"You think?"

"Nash, he could go crazy."

"Not when we bring him the prize," Nash said, "and here she comes."

He thrust the binoculars into Macchio's hands. When Macchio trained them on the spot, Nash indicated he saw a 4x4 Jeep moving in their direction and recognized it as the vehicle Cooper and the woman had been in when they had been at the crash site.

"That's the vehicle registered to Laura Devon," Nash said. He fired up the SUV.

WHEN LAURA DEVON'S 4x4 came around the last bend before the approach to Hardesty, she was forced to slam on her brakes to avoid crashing into the big, black SUV parked across the road. Two armed men were waiting in front of the SUV, weapons aimed directly at her. She recognized them both as men from the facility.

Her first instinct was to reverse away until common sense took over. There was no way she could avoid any shots fired at her. The road was too narrow for her to make a fast turn. She sat and stared at the armed pair. One of them stepped out of the SUV and pointed his SMG at her.

"Get out and walk over to us," Nash ordered. When she hesitated he raised his voice. "Let's go."

Devon opened her door and stepped out of the Jeep. She held her hands clear of her sides as she walked toward the SUV. Macchio opened a rear door for her to get in.

"I don't believe it," Devon said. "This already happened once before."

Nash smiled. "Déjà vu. We missed you. The invitation stands. Your room's still available. We've a way to go and this weather isn't getting any better. Time to move."

Macchio watched as Nash got the woman settled in the rear seat, then joined her.

"Let's get out of here," Nash said.

Macchio swung the SUV around Devon's abandoned car and they headed back along the road.

"Don't plan any trips to Vegas," Macchio said over his shoulder. "You're on a losing streak right now."

"It must be down to the company I keep running into."

She slumped against the back of the leather seat. Her thoughts were centered on Cooper. She knew he was determined to return to the facility to face Rackham. That concerned her. He still hadn't recovered 100 percent, and for what he was contemplating that could prove his undoing. During her short time with him, he had proved his capabilities. At his peak he would have handled matters with ease—but right now Matt Cooper was *not* at his best. The people he would be going up against wouldn't allow him any consideration for that. They would use anything to put him at a disadvantage.

And that would include using her as a pawn.

10

"I don't like all this waiting around," Roger Conklin said. "Where are these mothers?"

His partner, Sid Groesch, used to Conklin's grumbling, ignored him. He flexed his shoulders under the heavy raincoat. He wouldn't admit it, but Conklin had a point. It had been a long wait for Rackham's buyer.

"They'll show. Rackham called it, so they'll come."

"Yeah? What if they come out shooting? Tell me who gets hit first?"

"This isn't the O.K. Corral," Groesch pointed out.

"Easily said. We know those Koreans are pissed the way the first deal went sour. Might be they'll want the merchandise without paying. Kind of revenge for almost getting screwed before."

"I don't think so. They won't want to blow away their supplier. From what I've heard, if they fuck about with Rackham, there won't be any chance if they want seconds."

"Yeah? Well, I don't think Rackham is the hotshot he makes out to be. If he's such an ace, how come he almost let that FBI undercover guy walk in and nearly screw the operation? Answer me that."

"As long as he foots the payroll, I don't give a damn if he's Daffy Duck. I'm in this for the money, not a merit badge."

Conklin lapsed into a sullen silence. He stared across the empty landscape, watching a thin mist of rain spiraling in off the low hills. He slung his SMG, thrusting a hand inside his raincoat and pulling out a pack of cigarettes. He lit one with a disposable lighter and sucked in smoke.

"Chopper comin' in," Groesch said, pointing at the jagged line of wooded hills. Conklin followed his partner's finger and made out the dark outline of a medium-size helicopter coming their way.

"About damn time," he muttered.

Groesch banged his fist on the metal door behind them. When the door opened and Rackham appeared, Groesch said, "Looks like they're here."

The helicopter, a silver-and-black Sikorsky, swung in over the concrete and settled. The rotor wash created a spray of rain that bounced off the front of the building and soaked the two men outside.

"Son of a bitch," Conklin yelled.

The whine of the chopper's engine wound down. The passenger door opened, and two men stepped out of the aircraft and ran to the building. Rackham stood just within the opened door, and he ushered the two North Koreans inside.

"Doing a good job, guys," Rackham said to Conklin and Groesch as he walked by.

The door slammed shut.

"The more I see that jerk the less I like him," Conklin said.

RACKHAM SHOOK HANDS with his guests and led them to the enclosed office structure at the side of the building.

"After our last unfortunate episode, I decided this would be safer," he said. "Less chance of being seen."

The lead North Korean, his face impassive, simply nodded. His name was Jun. There was no more to his title than that.

The second Korean, no name at all for him, said, "We should conclude our business as quickly as possible."

"Fine," Rackham said. "I understand your caution."

"We *need* the virus," Jun said. "But what happened gave us concern."

"The FBI, according to my sources, was hoping that by placing a man undercover they would locate our facility. We dealt with him before he was able to transmit any findings back to his people." Rackham passed over a flash drive. "You'll see what I mean when you view the recording."

Jun managed a smile when he realized what Rackham meant.

"How did the entrapment come about?" Jun's man asked.

"The FBI try as many means as they can to make an arrest. The sting operation was one of them. By a miscalculation someone from another agency found out and walked in when our man was making the deal. The man who was impersonating one of your people was shot as well as our representative."

"A messy affair all around," Jun said.

"Have you found your missing man?"

Jun shook his head. "He must have been intercepted after he journeyed to attend the meeting. We may never find his body. If he does still live, we will deal with him. Failure is not an option we favor."

"In truth no one really profited from the meeting."

"So you will be able to complete our order?"

"Yes. Within the next twelve hours I've been told. When that's done, we'll abandon the current facility and relocate elsewhere. I'll give you the location and we can conclude our negotiations." Rackham smiled. "Business goes on, gentlemen."

He indicated the case sitting on the small table. Jun crossed to it and snapped the lid open. The glass vial rested in the sponge lining. Jun inspected it carefully before closing the lid and securing the catches. He picked up the case and nodded to his companion. The man handed over the leather bag. Rackham placed it on the table without even checking the contents.

"Once we have analyzed the item I will contact you," the

nameless man said. "Our man is capable of analyzing the sample in a few hours." He glanced at the bag handed over to Rackham. "You do not wish to inspect the contents?"

"Do I need to?" Rackham said. "This is about trust between us. We both want a successful outcome. How would betrayal benefit anyone at this stage?"

"Have the consignment ready as soon as possible. We wish to move the operation forward. Our timetable has been advanced."

"Have a safe journey," Rackham said.

He escorted the two North Koreans to the door and stood watching as they returned to the waiting helicopter. As the rotors began to turn, Rackham told Conklin and Groesch to step inside. Conklin closed the door as the displaced rain slapped against the building.

"Time to get out of here," Rackham said.

"First good thing I heard all day," Groesch stated.

Rackham walked by and went inside the office. He was standing at the table, his back to Conklin and Groesch as they joined him.

"At least we got the money this time," Conklin said, starting to feel a little less aggrieved.

"Yeah," Groesch agreed. It made getting soaking wet worth it.

"When do we get paid?" Conklin asked.

"Right now," Rackham said.

He turned around, his right hand coming out from under his jacket with a P226. He fired without hesitation. The first slug took Conklin between the eyes; the second hit Groesch just above his left eye. They hit the floor together. Rackham stepped forward and stood over their jerking bodies. He deliberately fired two more 9 mm slugs into their heads, the through and through shots removing the backs of their skulls and spreading bloody brains across the floor.

Rackham slipped his cell phone from his pocket and keyed

in a number. When it was answered he said, "Come and get me out of here."

He took the bag and made for the door. He stood waiting and saw a large SUV roll into view. It sped across the concrete and came to a stop. Rackham stepped outside and pulled open the passenger door. The SUV swung around and picked up speed.

"Any problems?" the driver asked, glancing at the leather bag Rackham had placed between his feet.

"None worth mentioning," Rackham said.

He turned to look at the driver.

Lise Delaware moistened her curving lips as she concentrated on her driving. Her eyes gleamed with some inner thought.

"Groesch and Conklin? You're certain they're both dead?"

"Three shots each to the head," Rackham told her.

He heard the sharp inhalation as she savored the words, saw the way her hands gripped the wheel, the knuckles showing white with tension. Her smooth, flawless cheeks reddened with a noticeable flush.

"Good," she said, her voice husky.

"Most women get turned on by the sight of diamonds," Rackham said.

"I'm not *most* women."

That, Rackham had to agree, was the understatement of the decade.

Lise Delaware was the extreme in everything she said or did. From the way she dressed to her skills in the bedroom, the woman excelled. Rackham had sampled it all and always came back for more. He enjoyed her company, and he found her organizational abilities second to none. Within the group she held a position of power that allowed her to dominate her male colleagues. Some didn't like that, but they never questioned her position. Delaware was top echelon, and if she continued to endorse Rackham there was no one who would voice a complaint.

"Cooper?" she said quietly, changing the subject. "Where do we stand with him?"

Rackham reached up to touch the still-raw gouge around his neck under the turtleneck sweater he wore. The wound still hurt, and he had promised himself he would exact some revenge for what Cooper had done to him.

"Bastard is still evading us. Staying one step ahead. He'll want to take us down. No question."

"Greg, we have to get our hands on him. If he talks to the right people, it could all go up in smoke. The government will make us disappear."

"Think I don't know? Lise, please don't start quoting Code 18 at me. I understand it well enough."

"If we get away with this, we'll have money to burn. If we don't and they catch us, it's goodbye to sunny days and green grass. They'll bury us so deep we'll never need sunshades again. Alternatively we could be executed."

"I always did admire your way with words," Rackham said.

"Then we need to find Cooper."

"That's why I'm cutting off outside links so we don't have strays hanging around."

"Like Groesch and Conklin?"

"They were just guns for hire. Not really part of the main team. We couldn't afford to have them running around loose."

"So let's get your people back on Cooper's trail. Keep the production team working 24/7. If the Koreans like the sample, they'll be coming back for more. We need to be ready for them."

"We will be. The batch will be ready in hours. I look ahead, Lise. We have other interested parties. Even if the Koreans pulled out, we can offer the virus elsewhere."

"I do understand the concept, Greg, and I have impressed it on the organization. It's hard work sometimes. They have this innate ability to reduce everything down to dollars and cents without any thought that to make money you have to invest in time and patience."

"I'm not criticizing you, Lise. With this virus we have no choice but to be careful. Any break in protocol and we could end up like Pembury and the others." He smiled. "Though they *were* unwilling victims."

"We have that on our side. None of the group is going to come down and start banging on the door demanding to be let in. Those people are too scared to come within a hundred miles of the facility. They can whine and bleat all they want. As long as they run interference within their individual departments, we'll be fine. That will give us the stretch to do this properly before we pack our bags and move on."

"Counting the profits."

She smiled at him, dropping a hand on his thigh, her nails digging in. "Money isn't everything. I know enough to understand that."

Rackham's phone shrilled. He answered the call. Delaware turned her head slightly and caught a glimpse of the expression in his eyes. What she saw pleased her. When Rackham ended the call, during which he hadn't spoken a word, he glanced at her.

"That was Nash. It appears he has been using his initiative. He's retaken the woman who was with Cooper. He's returning her to the facility. It gives us an edge. Cooper will try to rescue the woman. When I spoke to Cody earlier, I told him how to handle it. Wound Cooper if they have to but don't kill him. I want that guy back."

"Call Nash back," Delaware said. "Get him to send a team to Hardesty. Get them to check out the place."

"Why?"

"A feeling. Just in case Cooper shows his face there. Let's cover all the bases. Send in a few men. We can spare them to look the place over. Humor me, Greg."

"Woman's intuition?"

Delaware shrugged. "Maybe. Then we can go to the safe-house knowing we're covered."

"If Cody does get his hands on Cooper, I can wait. In fact the longer I wait the more I'll enjoy it when I get around to dealing with him. We'll go to the backup house. As soon as the virus batch is ready it can be brought to us."

Delaware digested the information. "This is getting more interesting all the time."

"I get the impression all this is turning you on, Lise."

"You aren't wrong, love," Delaware said, her ragged tones an indication of her arousal. "If we have time when we make the deal, I'll be forced to show you just how much."

Rackham flinched slightly as her nails dug deeper into the flesh of his thigh, and for a few seconds he forgot about Cooper, the virus and the vast amount of money they were liable to make from the upcoming deal.

11

Joshua Riba had slowed the red SUV and swung it off the road, entering the parking area outside the diner. There were no other vehicles in sight. He cut the big V8 engine and sat scanning the area before he climbed out and locked the vehicle. He pulled his leather jacket over the holstered .45-caliber Colt Peacemaker revolver he carried in a cross-draw holster on his left hip, adjusted the fit of his black Stetson and made his way to the diner's entrance.

Standing over six feet tall, with a leanly muscled body, Joshua Riba was a full-blooded Apache from New Mexico. Apart from his white cotton shirt he was dressed in black, right down to his Western-style leather boots. He was a direct descendant of an Apache warrior called Charriba, a man who had fiercely resisted the coming of the white man and had fought a running battle with the U.S. Army. Riba still had family living in New Mexico, but they were peaceable and existed alongside the whites on their own terms. Riba was a fully licensed P.I., maintaining a good relationship with his people that helped combine the modern alongside the traditional.

He was here in Hardesty on a personal mission. Looking for the man he *now* knew as Matt Cooper. When Riba had first come into contact with the man he had used the name Belasko. That had been a while back during the Zero incident, when Riba had become involved in the affair and had sided with the man. Since then they had maintained a loose contact. In the short time they had worked together Riba had come to admire the enigmatic man.

Now he was looking for him. Cooper had vanished, and Riba had been drawn into searching for him by a man named Hal Brognola. Riba's association with Brognola had also been during the Zero affair.

Brognola's call on Riba's personal cell phone had come out of the blue, and the P.I. had picked up on the man's concern.

"I haven't heard from him in a while," Riba said. "Is he in trouble?"

"That's what I'm trying to figure out. He's off the radar."

"Not doing work for you?"

"No. He takes on assignments independently. I found out he was doing a favor for a colleague in Justice. The guy Cooper is looking for is FBI, and it's being kept low-key because there's a suspected security leak in the guy's department. The man Cooper is looking for may have been compromised. Cooper went after the agent, but it looks as if the mission has gone off the rails."

"Can't you trace him through his cell?"

"Tried but no luck. My friend told me the area he was working, so at least I can point you in the general direction. The last signal we picked up was somewhere in the Northwest. The nearest town of any size is called Hardesty, some little town way up from Seattle. But his cell has stopped transmitting completely."

"That's closer to me than your neighborhood," Riba said.

"Can't deny that was on my mind," Brognola said with a trace of embarrassment.

Riba laughed softly. "Does *Pinda Lickoyi* have a red face?"

"Maybe. He also has a missing friend, Joshua. I've tried my legitimate sources, but I haven't come up with anything yet by having to pussyfoot around."

"So now you're checking unofficial sources."

"Yeah."

"Let me try," Riba said. "Give me the source of his last cell signal and I'll put on my tracking moccasins and go take a look."

"You sure about this?"

"What the hell. Business is quiet and I don't like quiet."

"I won't forget this."

"Wait until you get my bill," Riba said.

"Give me an hour, and I'll have a chopper pick you up and fly you to Cooper's last known location. By the time you arrive, there will be a set of wheels waiting."

"Sounds good. Am I on expenses?" Riba said with a chuckle in his voice.

"Find Cooper and I'll add a bonus."

Just over an hour later Riba was buckled into the passenger seat of a chartered helicopter as it lifted off from New Mexico and quickly gained height. Riba had been ready by the time the chopper showed up. He had tossed in his gear, answering his cell phone even as the helicopter took off.

Brognola again.

"Nice timing," Riba said.

"We aim to please," the big Fed said. "When you touch down, a Chevy 4x4 will be waiting for you. Fueled up and ready to roll. You'll know which one it is because it's red. Just like the one you own."

RIBA OPENED THE DOOR and stepped inside the diner, looking around the near-empty place.

One man stood behind the counter. Another was perched on one of the stools, clad in denim work clothes, hunched over a steaming mug. Both men picked up on Riba's imposing figure as he crossed the diner and took a seat.

"Can I get you something?" the guy behind the counter asked.

Riba nodded. "Coffee would be good."

The other customer glanced at Riba.

"Long way from home, ain't you, Chief?"

Riba took off his hat and dropped it on the counter. He nodded.

"You might say that. Not much going on around here."

"Been that way since they built the new highway and killed the town."

Riba smiled at the old man. "That so?"

"Gets so he tells ever'body who comes in," Vern Mitchell said.

"If they'll listen," Sam Jarvis complained. He used an old man's hard-done-by tone. "All I'm sayin' is this town had a life before they took the traffic away. So we don't get many visitors of late. Only a few of the surviving locals and that's not many."

"Had that young couple in the other day."

"Ha," Jarvis snapped. "All they had time for was lookin' at each other. They only come in 'cause they got lost. Just before Cooper showed…"

Riba's head came up, his eyes fixing on the old man.

Behind the counter Mitchell sucked in a breath.

Sam Jarvis seemed to shrink under the P.I.'s gaze.

Riba took a long swallow of coffee and pushed his mug across the counter for a refill. He watched Mitchell top up the mug. Riba reached inside his jacket and took out his ID. He placed the opened black leather badge holder on the counter so both Mitchell and Jarvis could see it clearly.

"My name's Joshua Riba. I'm a licensed P.I. I work out of New Mexico. I'm here because I heard Matt Cooper might be in some kind of trouble. He's my friend. We worked together a while ago and covered each other's back. I'm here to do the same thing for him."

The silence stretched, Mitchell and Jarvis unsure how to take Riba's explanation.

"Kind of difficult for us right now," Mitchell said. "How do we know you aren't…?"

"Out to cause Cooper harm?"

Jarvis nodded. "See, the way things already played out, we don't know who we can trust."

"You saying Cooper's out on a limb?"

"Him and Laura both," Mitchell said hurriedly.

"Laura?"

"They took off together and we haven't heard from them since," Jarvis said.

"Hey, slow down," Riba said. *"Laura?"*

"Laura Devon," Mitchell said. "She works here. Kind of took your guy Cooper under her wing when he came in lookin' worse for wear."

"He hurt bad?"

"He come walkin' in through a rainstorm," Jarvis said. "It looked like he'd been through the wringer. Had a nasty clout on his head an' was in a bad way. Seems he was on the run from people trying to do him harm."

"And he was having some difficulty recalling who he was and why he was here," Mitchell said. "But he knew enough not to want to get us involved."

"How do you mean *difficulty?* Memory loss?"

Mitchell nodded. "Something like that. Now, Laura wouldn't have any of him leaving. He insisted but then he kind of lost it and collapsed. Laura has a room out back, and we helped carry him there and put him on her bed."

"Regular ministering angel," Jarvis added. "She was a medic in the military. Served her time on Afghanistan. She tended to him and made him stay put. He slept overnight, but come morning he said he had to move on. He was more concerned *we* might get into trouble if he stayed around. Hell, that boy worried more about our lives than he did his own."

That was Cooper, Riba thought. He had the capacity for thinking about others first, putting his own safety last if others were being exposed to harm.

"What happened then?"

"Come morning Cooper said he had to get moving. Laura brought her own car and insisted she drive him," Jarvis said. "He was still weak from whatever happened to him. Now, he was ready to take himself off on his own, but he saw sense in the end and they left in Laura's car."

"Where were they heading?"

"Cooper wanted to find out what happened to him. He has a regular bee in his bonnet about it. What was making him mad was he couldn't recall how things started out. He figured he crashed his vehicle a way back along the road. So he decided to start there."

Riba considered his options. There weren't many.

"Did either of them have a cell phone?"

"Laura took hers. He didn't have one when he came in," Jarvis said.

"You have her number?" Riba asked. "I can get it traced. Maybe give me some idea where they might be heading."

Mitchell and Jarvis looked at each other, still wary of Riba.

"If I can come up with tracing Laura's cell phone, so can the opposition," he said. "I can call a contact in Washington. He'll confirm who I am. And he can help track Laura's cell phone." A thought occurred to Riba. "Have there been any strangers around since this started? People checking the town? Unknown vehicles?"

"You said there were a couple out on the south road, Sam," Mitchell said. "That would be the stretch Cooper walked into town from."

Jarvis nodded. "That's right. I was driving out to see if I could spot Cooper's car. He said he'd run off the road a few miles back. Now, I did spot an SUV cruising the area. So I stayed out of sight."

"You get any ID from them?"

Jarvis shrugged. "Guess I'm not as sharp as I might have been," he said. "Only thought about it later."

"Don't fret about it," Riba said.

"Only thing I do recall. That SUV was black and had those tinted windows. You know, the kind you can't see through."

"Never do understand that," Mitchell said. "All black. Shaded glass. Folk are more likely to remember something like that. Or do they think it makes them invisible?"

"Go figure," Riba said. "Did you spot Cooper's vehicle?"

"I found it. It was off road like Cooper said, jammed up against a big old tree. The front was wrecked. It looked like somebody had already checked it out, too. And there were bullet holes in the thing. Looks like it took a few shots. Now, I did get details. Registration." Jarvis searched through his pockets. "Seems I put the details in here somewhere. Forgot all about it." He finally produced a folded paper, opened it up and handed it to Riba.

Keying his cell phone, Riba waited until the contact number wound its way through the secure channels. He recognized Hal Brognola's gruff voice.

"Riba," he said by way of identifying himself.

"You got something?"

"Maybe. Can you run a trace on this cell phone?"

Riba quoted the number and Brognola said, "We'll run it. Anything else you have to tell me?"

"I'm in Hardesty. Cooper *was* here. From what I've found out he was injured. Sketchy details but seems like he had some head trauma and his memory had been affected. His vehicle was abandoned. It had been in a collision with a tree and had some bullet holes in it. He walked quite a distance and ended up in Hardesty. He rested up overnight, then took off accompanied by a local woman who was driving him. The cell phone number belongs to her. If we run a trace, we might locate Cooper."

"I'll come back as soon as we have anything. Watch your back, Joshua."

"I always do."

"What the hell is going on up there?"

"You'll know when I do."

Riba ended the call. He toyed with the coffee mug, aware there was little he could do until Brognola called back—hopefully with information that would put him on Cooper's trail.

"This is one quiet town," Riba said.

"In the process of shutting down," Mitchell said. "Only a few of us left."

"The bridge leading to the interstate did for us," Jarvis said. "Left the town high and dry like I said."

"Hey, the man doesn't need telling."

"I don't mind," Riba said. "World moves on and places get left behind. That be the bridge I came over after I left the interstate?"

"That's right," Jarvis said with a satisfied smirk on his weathered face.

"Sam, why don't we put it all down on tape and you can sell copies whenever you get folk stopping for gas."

Jarvis stared at his friend. "Times are, Vern, I despair over you."

"You hungry?" Mitchell asked Riba. "I know Laura isn't here, but I can turn my hand to workin' in the kitchen. We got ham, steak and such."

"Sounds good," Riba said. "Hey, tell you what. I did some time in a kitchen once. Let me step back there and rustle us up something. Give me something to do." He walked around the counter and went through to the kitchen. "Nice setup. You bring me another coffee and I'm all set to go."

"You got it," Mitchell said.

TWENTY MINUTES LATER and the rich aroma of cooking meat wafted into the diner. Mitchell and Jarvis could hear Riba humming to himself as he cooked.

"You need any help back there?" Mitchell asked.

"Thanks, no."

Mitchell turned to speak to Jarvis. The old man had slid off his stool and was standing at the diner's front window. He was watching a black SUV easing along the street. It turned and rolled into the diner's parking lot, facing the building. It stopped and doors opened. Three men exited the vehicle.

"Riba," Jarvis called.

"Be ready in a minute," the P.I. replied.

Mitchell had seen the newcomers. He muttered under his breath as he saw the trio moving toward the front door.

"We got visitors," Mitchell said over his shoulder. "I don't think they've come for the chef's special."

Riba peered over the serving shelf and picked out the approaching trio.

"Let's see what they want," he said.

Mitchell heard the solid double-click as Riba dogged back the hammer on his Peacemaker.

"My insurance doesn't cover this kind of situation," Mitchell said.

The door opened and the three men walked into the diner. They separated as they crossed to the counter. Jarvis followed them and took his place on his regular stool.

"Morning, gents," Mitchell said. "What can I get you?"

The men were casually dressed. They could have been simply passing through if it hadn't been for the tight expressions on their faces or the sharp gleam of menace in their eyes.

"We're looking for a friend of ours. He came through town a day or so back," one of them said. "Might have been hurt."

"Car crash?" Jarvis asked innocently.

The speaker turned to stare at him. "What do you know about it, Pop?"

Jarvis bristled. "I'm not your *pop.* And I know about it because I run the gas station down the street. I might've taken a drive and seen the wreck."

"What else did you see?"

"Just a wrecked car. Nobody in it. That's all. *Sonny.*"

Mitchell could have yelled at the old man. He knew Jarvis was deliberately goading the man. Jarvis had a sharp tongue, and he didn't take crap from anyone. He tried to catch the man's eye but Jarvis pointedly ignored him.

"No one has been through town?"

"It isn't Times Square. We'd notice if a stranger showed up."

"So who belongs to the red SUV out there?" one of the other men asked. He turned to look at Riba's vehicle.

"Not that it's any of your business," Jarvis snapped, "but it's mine."

The guy gave a harsh laugh. "No way, old man—those wheels don't spell your name. Reckon your feet wouldn't even reach the pedals."

"Oh?" Jarvis bristled. "At least I *can* spell, *sonny.*"

A cold sensation rolled Mitchell's stomach. He saw it coming, but there wasn't a thing he could do.

The guy closer to Jarvis half turned his upper body. His left arm came with it, palm open, and he hit Jarvis across the side of his head. The blow landed square, the impact throwing the old man off his stool. Jarvis didn't even have time to yell as he dropped, hitting the diner floor hard.

"No way!" Mitchell yelled.

He reacted out of pure instinct, his right hand swinging the open-topped coffeepot. Steaming liquid erupted from the pot and hit the guy full in the face. He stepped back, screaming, his hands clawing at his raw flesh.

The guy who had first started asking questions reached under his open jacket and started to pull the pistol he had in a shoulder holster. He got the black SIG Sauer clear and turned it in Mitchell's direction.

The solid crack of Riba's .45 Colt Peacemaker drowned out every other sound in the diner as he leaned into view and fired.

The heavy slug hit the would-be shooter in the right shoulder, breaking bone as it cored in. The short range helped maintain the slug's velocity and it spun the target around. He stumbled and went down on his knees, clutching his bloody shoulder, his pistol dropping from numb fingers.

Riba burst into view from the kitchen area as the third man pulled his own weapon from his hip holster. It was a similar weapon to the one his stricken partner had wielded. He jerked it in the direction of the moving P.I., triggering a couple of shots that exploded crockery on the shelf close to Riba.

The P.I. hauled himself to a stop, leveling the big revolver, and put a pair of .45 slugs into his opponent. The guy stepped back, eyes widening with the shock of the impacts. Riba's accuracy placed both bullets over the guy's heart as they mushroomed through his ribs, splintering bone and tearing into the organ. He dropped without a sound.

Moving into the diner, Riba quickly collected the discarded weapons, reaching into the coat of the coffee-scalded guy and taking his. He tossed the guns on the counter. He made the now-moaning man sit on one of the barstools while Mitchell brought a clean towel soaked in cold water. He handed it to the man.

"Use it," Riba said. "Just don't make any stupid moves 'cause I still got loaded chambers here."

Then he said to Mitchell, "Go check Sam." When the man hesitated Riba snapped, "Do it now, Vern."

Riba took out his cell phone and dialed Brognola's number again.

"Time to work your magic," Riba said when the big Fed came on.

He ran Brognola through what had happened.

"Now I know why Cooper likes you," Brognola grumbled. "You're just like him."

"They weren't about to discuss things in a civilized manner," Riba muttered. "And thanks for the compliment."

"Okay. You need to stay where you are. Don't go running off before we clear this with the local law. Understand, Joshua? You take off and you could have a posse of law on your tail."

"I get it. But I don't want any trail going cold on me. Longer I'm held back…"

"I understand. Let's process this right."

"Anything on that cell phone yet?"

"I should have your questions answered soon. Just take it one step at a time."

"Can you arrange for some kind of presence here," Riba added, "in case these people come back? There's no reason this town should have to suffer because of these perps."

"Leave that with me, Joshua."

Riba ended the call and checked out Mitchell and Jarvis.

The old man had a nasty bruise on his cheek, but his fall from the stool had only shaken him up.

"That was some dive you took," Mitchell said as he got Jarvis back on his stool.

Jarvis waved off the incident. "Take more than a fall to finish me," he said.

His outward bravado didn't hide the slight tremble in his hands. His face was pale and waxy.

Mitchell went behind the counter and gathered fresh mugs. He picked up the second of his coffeepots from the hot plate and began to pour, then noticed how badly his hands were shaking.

"You let me do that," Riba said.

He had been checking out the man with the shoulder wound, wrapping towels from behind the counter around the guy's shoulder. He wiped his hands and took the pot from Mitchell, filling the three mugs.

"I never knew anything could happen so damn fast," Mitchell said.

"Something like that doesn't leave much time to think," Riba said. "It comes up quick and you take it on or the other guy wins. No second chances."

Jarvis clutched his coffee mug. "It's been a hell of a day so far. And we never got that food you were cooking."

"You still want to eat?" Mitchell asked.

Jarvis considered, then shook his head. "You're right. Sorry. I lost my appetite."

Riba smiled, glancing up from reloading his Colt. "What the hell, I'm not letting that good food go to waste."

He was still eating when his cell phone rang. It was Brognola.

"I've got the whole team working on this," the big Fed said. "Here's what we have. Laura Devon's cell phone is transmitting erratically. It's damaged. Maybe got wet. It's a stationary signal."

"Could be. You should see how bad the rain is up here."

"We did manage to pin down a partial location north of Hardesty. You have GPS on your cell phone?"

"Yeah."

"We'll send you coordinates. One of our people managed to pick up a satellite image from the location. It turns out it's an abandoned military facility that was decommissioned over thirty years ago, so there isn't a lot of intel on it. According to what we've found, it's been forgotten and just left to the environment, most likely taken over by the forest."

"What was it used for originally?"

"Details are sketchy but reading between the lines it must have been some kind of research facility. Likely that's why it's in such a remote area."

"Military and research. Not always a good mix," Riba said. "Nothing from Cooper's cell phone?"

"It's shut down and there's no more trace of it."

"Okay, I'll follow the woman's signal and see where it takes me."

"My team is still digging. If we come up with anything, I'll pass it along. Joshua, be careful. There's something wrong about all this."

"I already figured that."

"Helpful?" Mitchell asked as Riba ended the call.

"I've had better calls. But at least I got a direction to follow."

Riba gave Mitchell his cell phone number. The man promised he would pass along anything that came in.

The police arrived a little while later. It was obvious they had been given a heads-up on the local situation, and though they were slightly disgruntled they followed orders and gave Riba little hassle before taking the situation in hand. An ambulance showed up after another half hour.

By that time Riba had left, following the GPS track the cyberteam at Stony Man Farm had sent to his cell phone.

12

Riba had learned his tracking skills from his elders, his grandfather and even his great-grandfather before the old man had passed on. The tracking skills of the Apache were legendary. In the distant past it had been a tradition to pass on the old ways once a youngster reached the age of learning, and no Apache considered himself a man until he had acquired those skills.

Joshua Riba's classroom had been the New Mexico wilderness. Under the patient tutelage of his elders he had absorbed everything they had passed to him. Sights and sounds and smells. They all went before him, being absorbed, remembered, until they became as natural to him as breathing. He learned to read signs. How to analyze each small mark left by his quarry. He took on the ability to pick up scents. How to notice unusual sounds that were out of place. Riba learned well and he learned quickly. And none of the things he learned were ever forgotten. They served him well. Even when he became a military warrior and served in Iraq. He took his Apache lore with him when he became a P.I., using those well-taught skills in the environs of cities. His hunting expertise helped track when he was searching in the concrete canyons as much as it did in the desert.

Now he was employing those skills in order to find his friend. Cooper was on his own, up against enemies with little regard for human life. Riba knew the man was good, but he was less than at his best and that might place him at a slight disadvantage. Cooper was as much a warrior as Joshua Riba. Right now he needed someone with him to provide backup.

Riba found where Cooper had abandoned his vehicle, concealing it in a stand of trees. The hood still bore a little heat, indicating it had been left some time ago. The Apache picked up Cooper's tracks leading from his concealed SUV, and started to follow.

AN HOUR ON AND RIBA, checking his cell phone's GPS, realized he was in the vicinity of the facility.

It was at that same time he spotted the armed men moving in on Cooper's back trail. He melded into the undergrowth, becoming invisible as he stalked the stalkers.

The .45 revolver sat in its hip holster, held firm by the hammer loop. Riba slid his steel-bladed knife from the sheath on his belt, gripping the rawhide-bound handle in his right hand. He needed a silent kill here, could allow no mistakes that might alert others who were following Cooper.

Riba heard the guy before he was in striking distance. The man, armed with a pistol in a shoulder rig and an SMG, was speaking into a comm unit he was wearing. Riba heard enough of the conversation to confirm that Cooper was the intended target. He smiled to himself as he listened. The man was advertising his presence without a thought he might be overheard.

Riba closed in fast. He hadn't established just how strong the force was following Cooper. He did realize they were moving in. The sooner he started to reduce the odds the better.

Emerging from the deep shadows of the undergrowth, Riba saw the guy pause to adjust his comm unit, losing any caution he might possess. It became Riba's window of opportunity and he seized it. Two long strides and he was behind the man. He reached out and clamped his left hand over the guy's face, his fingers digging into vulnerable eye sockets. The instant agony took the guy's breath. Riba pulled his prey's head back, sweeping the razor-keen blade of his knife left to right across the throat, cutting deep. The surge of blood flooded down the guy's shirtfront, soaking it. Riba let go and the man sagged to his knees, his hands grabbing at his severed flesh, blood squirting between his fingers as he began to die.

Bending, Riba picked up the dead man's weapon. It was an FN P90 and a visual check showed him the translucent top-loading magazine held its 50-round, 5.7 mm load. The selector switch was in the full-auto position. The P90's modern styling had produced a compacted weapon that fit neatly into the shooter's hands.

Before he moved off, Riba rolled the body beneath a tangle of heavy brush. His silent kill maintained his unseen position. He took a moment to realign himself with Cooper's distant line of travel, then loped silently through the thick foliage and trees.

He understood there would be more opposition. Cooper was a sought-after target, and the enemy was throwing as much manpower into the field as possible.

Riba was here to even the odds and help his friend. He didn't give a damn how many there were. Cooper had stumbled onto something that needed his unique approach, and despite being impaired by the physical trauma he had suffered, the man was staying on mission. Riba was simply lowering the odds a little.

He moved forward as quickly as possible. Riba wanted to reach Cooper ahead of the enemy.

He was still unable to physically see Cooper. Yet he homed in on the man by following the faint trail Cooper left behind, small things that might have been easily missed by others. To Riba they stood out sharply.

He spotted a faint boot print on soft ground. The recent rainstorms had left the earth open to being marked as someone stepped by. They weren't fresh enough to have been made by the men following Cooper, but there was enough of the fading depression to point Riba in the right direction; once he had seen that boot print Riba knew to look out for others.

The opposition had left marks, too. They were haphazard, telling him the men were casting about in numerous directions where Cooper's stayed on line. He was moving in a single direction, not turning about and twisting as the others were. Riba smiled; Cooper knew where he was heading and maintained his forward line of travel.

Faint sound caught Riba's attention, a brief rustle that told him someone was close by. He crouched, staying in the shadows, homing in on the sound. His eyes sought out the perpetrator. He found the guy, not more than twenty feet to Riba's right. The tracker made out the lean figure, dressed in too-bright clothes for the occasion and carrying an FN P90. The guy wasn't entirely clumsy, but his stalking techniques needed improvement.

Pity you won't be getting the chance to improve them, Riba thought.

He started in the guy's direction, sliding through the undergrowth with barely a leaf disturbed. As he closed in on his target, Riba could hear the guy speaking into his comm unit.

"You can't raise Jacko. How the hell do I know what he's doing?" The guy nodded at a response. "We keep moving. Rackham wants this guy. *What?* Quit worrying about Jacko. If we lose Cooper, it'll be *our* asses on the firing line. Rackham is already going ape-shit because Cooper broke out and blew the hotel exchange. Let's not screw up ourselves."

Riba slid forward a few feet, bringing himself up close behind the guy. He eased the knife from its sheath for the second time. Even when he rose to his full height his target was still unaware of his presence. Riba reached his left arm around and clamped his big hand over the guy's mouth, preventing him from uttering a sound. His right swung the knife in a powerful stroke, burying it deep in the base of the skull, severing the spinal cord. Riba twisted the blade, completing the action, and the guy entered into a spasm that continued as Riba followed him to the ground. Without pause the P.I. yanked the guy's head back and swept the knife across his throat, cutting deep.

Sheathing his blade, Riba moved on, back to where he had seen Cooper's track, and picked up again. He saw other signs of Cooper's cautious passing: a broken leaf stem still fresh at the point where it had been snapped; more boot prints. Cooper was good, but in his current state of mind the man wasn't fully observing caution. If Cooper had been 100 percent operational, Riba would be having a harder time tracking him.

Riba thought ahead. If the men following Cooper realized they had lost a number of their team, they might contact base and advise. That could generate a backup squad moving out from the base to converge on Cooper from a forward position, putting him between two groups. It would lessen Cooper's chances. He wouldn't back off even if that happened. Riba knew the man's determination, a stubborn single-mindedness that wouldn't allow him to quit.

Picking up his pace, Riba closed the gap, wanting to reach Cooper before the opposing force was able to increase its strength. His eyes scanned the forest floor, locking onto Cooper's sparse trail. He noticed the boot prints were becoming wider spaced; Cooper was moving faster himself.

Twenty minutes brought Riba closer. There was less reduction in the prints, meaning Cooper wasn't far ahead.

He caught a fleeting glimpse of a figure: tall, broad shouldered, a flash of dark hair.

Riba increased his own pace now, losing a little caution as he powered through the foliage, ignoring the slap of errant tendrils against his face and body.

He heard a distant rumble of thunder. The first drops of a rain shower filtered through the high canopy of treetops. He suddenly thought of home, the dry New Mexico landscape.

It was becoming more appealing with every passing minute. A smile edged his lips.

And it was in that moment of lapsing concentration he was confronted by a dark shape stepping out in front of him. A powerful blow to his chest slapped him off his feet. Riba hit the sodden forest floor, briefly caught off guard.

He sucked air into his lungs, calling himself all kinds of a fool for dropping his guard.

He stared up at his attacker.

And recognized the face. Unshaved, showing some heavy bruises, but so recognizable. The piercing blue eyes were fixed on Riba. They held a distant expression.

The pistol in Bolan's hand was steady, the muzzle aimed at Riba's face.

"Cooper. It's Riba. Joshua Riba. We worked together once. You remember Zero. Doug Buchanan. Saul Kaplan. Think back. Clair Valens. Lady agent. I spoke to Brognola. He was worried because you seemed to have fallen off the radar. I tracked you to the diner at Hardesty. People there told me you showed up. Said you took a knock that skewed your memory. You weren't thinking too good… Vern and Sam."

Riba took a breath. He'd been talking fast to try to get through to Cooper. To at least give him some key words that might jog his memory. He had no idea if Cooper had recalled anything. The stare didn't waver—nor did the hand holding the pistol, so Riba remained motionless. It would take only a little pressure on the trigger to end it all.

Seconds passed.

It could have been a lifetime.

There was nothing in Cooper's intense stare to indicate whether he had understood what Riba had said.

And then there was a slight, but visible light of recognition in Cooper's eyes.

He mentally stepped back from whatever brink he was

standing on. Riba saw a change in his stance. The muzzle of the pistol lowered a couple of inches.

"You were Mike Belasko when I met you in Albany. We were working the same angle. Hal Brognola told me you changed your cover name. Matt Cooper."

"Joshua Riba? Colt .45 in a hip holster? Apache?"

Riba spread his hands. "Got it in one."

"You drove a big red truck."

"Still do."

"Brognola? Why do I recognize that name?"

"You work with him. Some deep-cover agency is all I know. You guys are real dark, and you have some clout."

"I know my real name but not much more."

"Keep the name to yourself. Must be a reason."

Bolan nodded. "Cooper, then."

Riba slowly climbed to his feet.

"So where do we go from here? The way you were traveling tells me there's a destination."

Bolan nodded. Riba was using words to jog Bolan's memory, to get his mind working.

"The place they were holding me earlier."

"Before you took off and ended up in Hardesty?"

"I've been on the move since then. There were guys after me."

"Still are," Riba said. "On our back trail right now."

"You figure how many?"

Riba shook his head. "Whatever number, it's less two."

Bolan smiled at the statement. "Did they wear comm units?"

Riba nodded.

"If they suffered losses, they might call home and pull in some more help."

Riba saw that even if he had lost some of his facilities, Cooper retained enough to stay alert to problems.

"I figured that, which is why I decided to speed up contact."

"Glad you did. What do we have ordnancewise?"

Riba held up the P90. "And I still have my trusty Peacemaker." He tapped the sheathed knife. "And this."

"The SIG," Bolan said, showing his pistol, "and a couple of extra mags."

"You got time to tell me why we're doing this?"

"Where we're heading is a lab that's producing a smallpox virus. The intention is to sell it to a North Korean client. I already quashed one attempt. This group won't give up. There's big money involved. I can't let them do it. I won't."

"That's enough to satisfy me."

Riba felt his cell phone vibrate. He took it out and answered. It was Mitchell.

"Problem," Mitchell said. "Cops just came in and told us they found Laura's 4x4 on the back road. Empty. No sign of her."

"Hold on." Riba turned to Bolan. "The woman. Laura."

"I sent her home. I didn't want her in any more danger. She was supposed to be heading back to the diner. Isn't she there?"

"No. Mitchell just told me the local cops located her car on the road. No sign of Laura."

Bolan stared at him for a moment. Then he nodded.

"Rackham's men picked her up. They'll bring her back to the facility to use her as a bargaining chip. They must know I'm coming for them."

Riba raised his cell phone. "I found Cooper," he said to Mitchell. "Laura was supposed to be on her way home. Looks like they picked her up."

Riba ended the call.

"How did the cops get involved?"

"We had unwelcome visitors at the diner. Looking for you, I guess. It got a little heated. After I called Brognola, he sent in the local law enforcement to handle things so I could go looking for you."

Bolan's face was set, his eyes cold with barely repressed fury.

"They made a big mistake, Joshua. They keep making them. This was their biggest and their last."

"So let's go start a war, friend."

13

The rain Riba had felt arrived with a vengeance. Far-off thunder continued, grumbling at a distance that rapidly closed in on Bolan and his companion. They heard it pounding the high cover of foliage, then the heavy downpour hit them. It was both a blessing and a hindrance. It covered their movements and drowned out any sound they might make; the reverse was the fact it did the same for the opposition. The enemy could move without being overheard, and visibility was reduced.

Mack Bolan felt at home in this environment. The discomfort from the rain was something he could tolerate. Even though he couldn't understand his affinity for this kind of terrain, he gained a degree of comfort from his surroundings.

He felt a light touch on his shoulder.

Riba.

"We got company. Your five o'clock. Two of them. Well armed. Three yards out. They don't see us."

Bolan nodded. He stopped, crouching, and Riba followed suit. They let the pair move on.

"No contact yet," one of them was relaying over his comm unit. "Yeah, we got that. Terminate on sight now..."

Riba leaned in close. "They must have spotted those two I dropped before I found you."

"They chose the game plan," Bolan said.

They allowed the hunters to move ahead before they slipped silently to the rear.

Riba hung the P90 around his neck by its strap, leaving his hands free. His final stride took him up to his target. He clamped a hand over the guy's face, yanking his head back so the throat was pulled taut. Riba's blade made its deadly pass, cutting deep. His prey made a wet gurgle of sound as he succumbed to the fatal slash.

The dead man's partner was drawn to the noise. He turned, bringing up his weapon. That was all he managed before Bolan snaked an arm around his throat. The soldier's other hand was placed, open palmed, against the guy's skull, pushing forward to complete the lock. With his air supply cut off, the man began to struggle. All he did was use up what oxygen remained in his lungs.

Bolan arched back, lifting his adversary off his feet, adding more pressure to his choke hold. The guy's struggles continued. There was no way he could free himself from Bolan's grip. It was ended quickly.

The Executioner lowered the limp body to the ground. He retrieved one of the abandoned P90s and an extra magazine, tucking it behind his belt.

Both bodies were searched. They carried no ID. No cell phones. Their only communication link came from the comm units they wore.

"Who are these guys?" Riba asked. "Ex-military? Private security?"

"Right now," Bolan said, "your guess is as good as mine. Whoever they are, they're mixed up in a dirty deal."

"No argument there."

"It's time we shut down this operation." Bolan faced his partner. "What they're working with is deadly material. It doesn't have any favorites. Get exposed, there's no turning back the clock."

"My shaman told me I have a long lifeline. This is not my time."

Bolan smiled. "Let's hope he was reading from the right page, Joshua."

"You must have faith. And anyhow, the shaman is my uncle. On my mother's side. Would he not tell the truth to his favorite nephew?"

Bolan checked the P90.

"Let's do this."

THEY MADE THEIR WAY through the thick undergrowth, drenched by the rain and aware there were still members of Rackham's team out looking for them. The forest floor underfoot was shedding water. It had absorbed as much as it was able. Now it pooled and created runoffs. Thunder was grumbling overhead. In the far distance the occasional flash of lightning illuminated the sky.

Bolan's hand reached out to stop the P.I. He made a quick gesture, indicating moving shapes ahead: an armed pair of gunners in camou outfits, wielding automatic rifles. They were approaching from the opposite direction. They had come *from* the home base.

"I see them."

Without a word Bolan pressed his upper body against the wide trunk of a tree, using it to steady his aim as he raised the P90. He slid the fire selector switch to semi-auto. Bolan's finger eased back on the trigger, and he sent a tight two-shot burst at the closer man. The 5.7 mm slugs took the guy in the high chest, punching into his heart. The gunner toppled back without a sound.

His partner swiveled with surprising speed, opening up on full-auto, lacing Bolan's area with heavy fire. The Executioner had dropped to a crouch the moment he fired, using the thick base of the tree as protection. The air was filled with eruptions of bark and raw wood as the long burst hammered the timber.

Riba had moved away from Bolan's position, allowing him precious seconds to settle his own aim. He hit the shooter sideways on, and laid down a long burst that ripped into the guy's body. He was kicked off his feet by the high-velocity impact of the slugs.

By the time Bolan and Riba reached the bodies, the heavy downpour had washed away most of the blood. They cleared weapons away from the men; the move wasn't necessary, as they were both dead. It was purely a reflex action.

With the knowledge that additional teams were in pursuit, Bolan and Riba moved quickly, pushing their way through the increasingly dense forest. The terrain began a slight rise in elevation. Bolan recalled his flight from the base, the downslope that had allowed him to build up speed quickly.

Beside the Executioner, Joshua Riba moved at an effortless pace. The P.I. appeared to possess limitless energy, enabling him to match Bolan's own dogged rate of travel. He focused on the way ahead, concentrating on the immediate task.

The crackle of autofire drowned out the rainfall. The air was filled with shredded greenery as slugs tore through.

Bolan crouched, seeking the source of the gunfire. Off to his side Riba made an angry sound and fell out of sight.

Bolan stared ahead, his eyes scanning the area, and spotted movement.

A man slipped into view, closely followed by a second.

They both wielded automatic weapons.

Riba's going down seemed to encourage them, and they lost some caution as they hurried forward.

Bolan let them come, then caught them as they stepped into an open area, the muzzles of their weapons probing the air.

He let them advance so they were fully exposed.

Then he tracked in the P90 and hit them on full-auto.

The men jerked as the 5.7 mm slugs hit home, tearing into clothing and the flesh underneath. Bolan arced his weapon's muzzle between the two, stitching them with a sustained burst. The pair turned and twisted as the slugs cored into them, tearing at flesh and spraying blood. There was no chance for them to retaliate. The pair tumbled to the ground, blood spurting as they fell. Bolan took a moment to replace the mostly spent magazine.

He turned to where Riba had fallen and saw the man kneeling on the sodden ground.

"Joshua? Were you hit?"

"Only in my wallet," Riba said. "Another damned jacket ruined."

He twisted his arm to show Bolan where a slug had sliced the sleeve of his leather jacket. His fingers were red with blood where the offending projectile had grazed his flesh.

"I thought it was serious," Bolan said.

"You think this isn't serious?" Riba grumbled. "Brother, I go through so many jackets in this business. Be cheaper to have my own herd of cows standing by."

"At least it's got you to practice ducking."

Riba made a mumbled retort as he bent over the bodies and retrieved extra magazines for the P90s. He handed one to Bolan.

"Let's move," Riba said.

A heavy roll of thunder followed as they made their way up the slope. They were hammered by the rain. It had increased to torrential proportions now. It made spotting moving figures harder.

"There," Bolan said, indicating the chain-link fence cutting through the landscape west to east of their line of travel.

"How did you get through?" Riba asked.

They were crouched in the tall grass, shadowed by trees. The metal fence looked unbroken despite having a substantial growth of creeping foliage curling around the links.

"I had an escort," Bolan said. "They brought me in through the gate."

"Easy way in."

"It didn't feel that way at the time."

Bolan indicated the direction they needed to go.

It took them almost five minutes to reach the gate. Still concealed in the undergrowth, they studied the gate and the empty gatehouse set to one side. There were no signs of cameras mounted at the gates, or set farther inside the fence. Some fifty feet back from the entrance was the hazy outline of the facility's main building. Dark and austere, it had the unmistakable look of a military installation.

"They're not going to invite us in," Riba said.

Bolan nodded in agreement. "Then we'll have to invite ourselves, Joshua."

He had picked up the sound of an approaching vehicle. Bolan tapped his partner on the shoulder. The P.I. glanced downslope and saw the dark bulk of an SUV. It slowed as it neared them. The gates were still open, as they had been when Bolan had made his break.

Crouching low, Bolan and Riba ducked inside the compound at the rear of the SUV as it rolled forward through the gates. Once they were inside the perimeter fence, they peeled away from the vehicle, left and right, flattening to the ground at the base of the fence. The SUV pulled away across the compound and stopped near the entrance to the facility. Three men climbed out. They moved to the main door and went inside the building. Bolan crawled to rejoin Riba. The encroaching foliage growing through the fence provided cover as they discussed their strategy.

"I need to locate Laura and get her out of this place. And find out exactly what Rackham and his crew are doing."

"You want to split up?" Riba asked. "We can cover more ground."

"Just remember this is a tough crew."

Riba grinned. "I wouldn't have it any other way. And I want to get out of this damn rain."

14

Bolan ducked through the door, moving forward. The trio from the SUV, ahead of him, heard the sound of his entry and turned, expecting to recognize a familiar face rather than an enemy's. By the time they realized their error, Bolan's P90 was on its tracking sweep. He fired the second he gained his first target, the stuttering crackle of autofire loud inside the building.

Bolan arced the muzzle left to right, the 5.7 mm slugs pounding into flesh and fracturing bone. The engagement lasted seconds. The three men tumbled to the floor in a mist of blood, weapons spilling from their fingers. Still on the move, Bolan delivered final short bursts that ensured none of the men would be getting up again.

From his earlier incarceration, Bolan remembered where Rackham had kept him and Laura. He moved down the branch corridor. Partway along he picked up the slap of running feet behind him, raised voices as the downed trio was discovered. As he registered the sounds, Bolan was ejecting the partly used magazine and slotting in a fresh one. With the P90 loaded and cocked, he swung in close to the wall and dropped to a crouch.

A pair of shooters rushed into view, weapons up and ready. For a few seconds they saw only an empty corridor. They lost any chance to gain the advantage when they spotted Bolan crouched at the base of the wall. His finger was already easing onto the SMG's trigger, the muzzle covering them. The FN cut loose, a stream of shell casings ejecting as the weapon fired.

Bolan caught a glimpse of the lead guy twisting to the side as the burst of slugs ripped at his throat and jaw. His scream of pain was cut off as the lower half of his face vanished in a welter of bloody flesh and shattered bone. His partner stumbled over him. The soldier caught the guy before he was able to recover and dealt him a long stream of slugs to his chest. The guy slumped against the wall, then slowly sagged to the floor.

The Executioner straightened, turning away from the dead and continuing along the corridor.

He was hoping he would locate Laura Devon in one of the rooms and not across the facility in the lab where the virus was being developed.

Bolan saw the door at the end of the corridor and recalled it was where he had been held. When he reached the first of the doors lining the corridor he raised a foot and kicked it open, stepping up close to check it out. Apart from a bed the room was clear. Bolan repeated the move on the next door with the same result.

He was turning away from the open door when he sensed a moving shape closing in on him.

Before he could react, a powerful backhand blow slammed across his cheek, knocking Bolan off his feet. He hit the floor, the P90 jarred from his hands. A large man hovered over him. One big hand caught hold of his shirt, dragging him upright. Bolan felt the SIG Sauer being yanked from his belt and cast aside.

"You won't be needing that."

Bolan recognized the voice even before he saw the face. *Cody.*

"Good of you to come back," the man said. "I still hurt from the whack you gave me with that shotgun. And Rackham wants you. He's the boss and he said alive, but that doesn't mean I can't hurt you first. I owe you."

Cody's heavy fist cracked across Bolan's jaw, spinning him back as his adversary let go of his shirt. He hit the wall and rebounded in Cody's direction. In his dazed state Bolan still understood what was happening. Cody would simply toy with him until he decided he had extracted enough payback. If Bolan failed to gain the upper hand, Cody would beat him senseless before he delivered him to Rackham.

"You feeling the pain yet?" Cody asked. "You feeling the fucking pain?"

Bolan decided he wasn't going to get into a war of words with the man. It would serve no purpose. He didn't respond and saw the expression in Cody's eyes change. Bolan's objective was to get to where they had Devon. The way was blocked by Cody, and the soldier needed to focus on taking the guy down as quickly as possible.

Cody was big, with a powerful build. Solid. He was no lightweight, and that could work to Bolan's advantage. Because of his sheer physical bulk, Cody wouldn't be fast. And physically powerful didn't mean invincible. There were parts of the body vulnerable on any man, large or small.

"Let's go, Cooper, you mother. Beating you stupid is going to be a real pleasure."

Bolan moved forward, feinting an attack, and as he closed in on Cody he watched the man's response. He was able to avoid Cody's massive fists as they swung left and right. Avoiding those large hands was a priority. Bolan ducked under the loose, slow swings. Before he stepped back, the Executioner launched a calculated kick that hammered in at Cody's groin. The big man grunted in agony as the hard kick slammed against his testicles. No amount of muscle building was going to make that part of his anatomy invulnerable. Cody hunched over, cupping his injured testicles.

As Cody's massive shoulders drooped, lowering his head, Bolan moved in again. He dropped his hands to the back of his opponent's skull and pushed down hard. Before the man could take defensive action, Bolan's right knee drove up in a brutal sweep, connecting with the man's face. Cody howled in pain as Bolan's knee smashed full into his face. The force shoved him upright, a glistening fan of blood and mucus streaming from his torn mouth and crushed nose.

Bolan launched a repeat kick that sank his booted foot into Cody's groin again, delivered to maximize the pain. This time Cody let out a loud wail. He used the pain to push himself at his tormentor, no pretense of any style; he was simply a hurt man going for the source of his agony. His momentum carried him directly into Bolan's path. The Executioner ducked low, hammering a clenched fist into Cody's left side, over his ribs.

Despite the taut muscle, Bolan's fist made a telling impact. As Cody stumbled past, Bolan slid to the floor, hooked his left foot around Cody's ankle, then made a pile-driving kick with his right foot against the side of Cody's knee. He heard a crunch as the joint collapsed, saw Cody's leg bend at the joint. The man lost his balance and went down, and Bolan rolled, pushing up to straddle his adversary's back, his arms coiling around his neck. Bolan levered hard, locking his grip around the thick neck to shut off the man's air supply. Cody began to thrash about, trying to reach back and get a grip on Bolan, but his muscled arms were not as flexible and he couldn't reach. Bolan snugged his head down against Cody's, increasing the pressure and ignoring the discomfort from his own injuries. Cody's struggles eventually ceased, his body becoming limp, and he dropped to the floor. When Bolan finally released his grip there was no further response from the man. He laid his fingers against the side of Cody's neck. There was no pulse. He pushed to his feet, his body taut from the effort. He felt the sting from his aggravated hip wound and felt the warmth of blood oozing from beneath the plaster. The side of his face and jaw ached from Cody's blows.

Bolan retrieved his weapons. He stepped through the door Cody had exited and negotiated the empty corridor. Doors to a number of the rooms were open. The soldier checked out each one. They were all empty. Midway along he saw that the door ahead was closed, the outer bolt in place. He slid the bolts back and swung the door wide, the P90 tracking into the room.

There was a bed with restraining straps. Devon was on the bed. She was struggling against the restraints as the door opened. She was ready to keep fighting until she recognized Bolan. The first thing he saw was the discolored bruise across her right cheek and the bloody cut in her lower lip.

"Matt?"

"Are you hurt?"

"Apart from being knocked about by that ape Cody, I'm pretty well okay."

Bolan unfastened the wrist restraints, then the broader straps around her chest and waist. Devon sat up, shaking her head.

"What?" he asked.

"This is the second time you've had to spring me from this place, Matt."

"What can I say. Let's go."

"Promise I don't have to ever come back here."

"Okay."

Devon followed him out the door and along the passage. When they reached the spot where Cody lay, Devon stepped around him.

"Now, there was a guy who had no idea how to treat a lady."

Bolan handed her the pistol from his belt. "Am I safe to put this in your hands? Or are you still mad at me?"

"Never mad, Matt. Just a tad upset." She spotted the blood soaking through from his hip. "How did that happen?" She saw Bolan glance down at Cody. "Oh. In that case…"

"We tangled a little."

The distant rattle of autofire reached them. It came from farther in the building, and Bolan figured Riba had to be involved.

"Stay behind me."

"You don't want me to take point?" Devon asked. She sounded disappointed.

Bolan led the way and they skirted the entrance door, turning onto the corridor on the far side. They soon reached a heavy steel door with a view port set at head height. There was a hazardous-materials sign on the door. Bolan could see the door was open.

The echo of more autofire crackled from beyond the door. A man called out. Through the view port Bolan caught sight of an armed figure moving into view from a side corridor. He was firing back at unseen gunners, then crouching as his shots were returned. He backed away, starting along the corridor in the direction of the steel door.

"Stay back," Bolan warned Devon as he gripped the edge of the door and dragged it fully open. Despite its bulk and weight, the door moved smoothly and easily on balanced hinges.

The retreating guy became aware of the opening door and turned to face it. His expression turned from relief to hostility when he realized Bolan wasn't one of his buddies.

"...the hell are you?" he yelled, then simply turned his SMG in Bolan's direction and fired in reaction.

Bolan had already turned his body aside, flattening against the thick doorframe. He felt the vibration as slugs struck the frame inches from his head. The soldier leveled the P90, tracked the moving gunner and eased the trigger back. The SMG flamed a burst of slugs that caught the guy in midstride. The target's midsection was punctured in a half-dozen places. He stumbled, then dropped to his knees, triggering his own weapon in a reflex action that drilled a burst into the ceiling. Bolan triggered a second volley, 5.7 mm slugs opening the gunner's throat in a burst of lacerated flesh. The guy arced backward, slamming to the floor, jerking for long seconds before his system shut down.

Bolan waved Devon in behind him as he went through the

door and advanced along the corridor. Like the area where he had been held, the corridor was lined with doors; the difference here was that each door had a thick view port set in it, and bore the hazard-materials warning.

"What the hell is this place?" Devon asked as she shadowed Bolan along the corridor.

"You might regret asking that question," Bolan said. "Especially if you learn the answer."

The side corridor angled off to the right. A sprawled and motionless body lay on the floor. There were more doors. The passage ran for around twenty feet before it terminated in yet another heavy door. This one was wide-open, with a second door no more than ten feet beyond.

"That one looks suspiciously like an airlock setup," Devon said. "Let's hope whatever they have in there is secure."

Bolan saw blood smears on the smooth, unbroken floor on the far side of the inner door. There was a bloody handprint on the gleaming metal of the door's edge. And a few more feet inside lay another body, a weapon close by.

There was movement farther along the corridor. Someone was flitting past a mass of wheeled cabinets. The movement caught Bolan's attention. He was certain he had recognized a black leather jacket and white shirt.

"Joshua? Is that you?"

The welcome response reached him from the depths of the gleaming white room.

"Cooper? 'Bout time you showed." Riba's tall shape eased into view. "You're covered. The place is clear."

Bolan moved to meet the P.I. Riba nodded, glancing beyond Bolan at Devon as she stepped forward.

"You're Laura? Are you okay?" he asked her.

Devon nodded, her cheeks flushing at his solicitous concern. "Yes. Confused, but fine."

"Always gets confusing when Cooper is involved."

"I've found that out the hard way."

"This is Joshua Riba," Bolan said.

"Met your friends at the diner," Riba said. "They've been worried about you.

"I got a wounded guy along here," Riba added.

He led the way back to where a man lay against the wall, clutching at a bloodied shoulder. The guy was in obvious pain. Devon knelt by him and eased his hand away from the wound, speaking to him in low tones.

"Shoulder bone is shattered," she said after a brief inspection.

Riba glanced at Bolan.

"Afghanistan," the Executioner explained. "She was a medic."

"Yes, I remember Jarvis mentioning that to me. Handy to have around."

Bolan stood over the ashen-faced man. "We'll get you help as soon as you give me what I need to know," he said. "Where's Rackham?"

"I'd tell him," Devon said. "He won't quit asking if you don't."

"He took off once he figured things were getting out of control," the man said.

"He have the virus?"

The guy nodded, grimacing as Devon maneuvered his arm into a secure position.

"It's on the way to him. One of the lab techs got the call to deliver it to him before they took off. Rackham's got the Koreans flying in from over the border."

"One more question and I'll call for medical help," Bolan said.

But the guy passed out before the question could be asked.

Devon checked him out and shook her head. "He's just lost too much blood," she said. "Shock from the pain isn't helping."

She made her way to the row of medical cabinets.

"Damn," Bolan said. "We need to get a line on where Rackham went."

Bolan followed Riba to the airlock doors and stared through the view window.

"This is the worst part," Riba said. "I took a look before you showed up. It isn't pretty."

Bolan examined the half-dozen cubicles. Even from where he stood he could see that each cubicle held a hospital-type bed and five of the beds held an occupant. A cursory glance showed him the cubicles were sealed, with overhead air and filtration units fitted. The cubicles held monitoring equipment and were brightly lit. Bolan could hear the hum of electronic machinery.

"Those cubicles must be isolated so the lab techs could work safely," he said.

All of the patients were restrained with wrist and ankle straps. Monitoring leads and plastic tubes led from each figure back to machines and fluid bottles. Flickering lines danced back and forth across readout panels.

Bolan checked the clipboards that hung outside the cubicles. He knew two out of the five people in the beds.

The third one along was Dr. Lawrence Pembury.

The one at the far end read *Bremner*. The man Bolan had been searching for.

Bolan wouldn't have been able to identify the man by his features. His face was disfigured by a mass of raw pustules covering his flesh. The pustules also covered his exposed arms and hands. Bremner's lips were swollen and bloated, his tongue, too. Many of the pustules had burst, allowing trails of thick pus to leak out. There had been hemorrhaging of blood from the man's eyes, nose and ears. Bolan could see that Bremner's chest was barely moving and the readouts on the monitoring equipment were close to being flatlined.

"What have they done to these people?" Devon whispered.

She had come up behind them to stare through the view window.

"They used them as guinea pigs. Test subjects for the damned virus they developed," Bolan said. The rage building up inside him threatened to explode. He felt Devon's hand grip one of his own.

As he moved along the line of cubicles, Bolan noted that the three other patients were dead. Their deformed bodies were massively infected, the burst pustules completely covering them. Rigid hands clutched at the empty air, the finger joints grotesquely swollen.

Gazing closer at Pembury's cubicle, Bolan saw that the doctor's symptoms were less advanced than any of the others. His glistening flesh showed pustules that were smaller in size, and only a few had burst. His face was turned toward the glass front of the cubicle and he caught Bolan's gaze, recognizing him. His swollen lips moved silently, one clawing hand raised in Bolan's direction. His eyes, weeping red, pleaded for some kind of relief.

The man's suffering tore at Bolan. For one of the few times in his life, he was unable to relieve the suffering of a victim. His hand closed even tighter around Devon's hand and she became aware of his feelings. Her free hand reached up to grip his arm.

"God help them," Bolan whispered because *he* couldn't. "I'll find Rackham. I don't care where he goes. I'll find him and make him pay for what he's done to these poor bastards."

He got Brognola's number from Riba and placed a call.

15

Bolan had spoken to Hal Brognola, Barbara Price and Aaron Kurtzman. His memory loss denied him full recognition, though there were flickers of memory. The fact he had a sometimes-intimate relationship with Price failed to rekindle a spark at the time; in truth it impacted more on the feisty young woman than she herself offered to show. Brognola understood her feelings when she realized Bolan didn't know who she was.

"We checked out the facility and it's been shut down," Bolan said. "Rackham left behind a defensive team and infected patients."

"He sounds like a nice guy."

"Riba and I need to go talk to Callum," Bolan said. "I'm sure he'll know where Rackham is. We need to track down Rackham ASAP, before he hands over that virus to the Koreans."

"You guys need to be checked before you leave," Brognola said. "And I'll get Bear to run a trace on this Greg Rackham, Striker."

"This place is near enough deserted except for the patients and a few of Rackham's crew. The lab technicians have gone, as well. Hell, they just left their victims strapped in those damned cubicles. Rackham is running a business. Dirty it may be, but he needs to keep his clients happy if that's the right way of describing it," Bolan said. "And what's this *Striker* about?"

"One of your code names," Brognola said. "And it's what you do."

"Do I have many code names?"

"How long have you got?"

"And we're friends?"

"Hell, yes. From way back. You don't recall that?"

"There's a snatch of memory about you chasing me and wanting to put me in jail. Is that accurate?"

"Yeah. Back in our early days. But things have changed since then."

"And we *still* like each other?"

The incongruity of the remark drew a genuine bellow of laughter from Brognola. When he regained control he said, "It goes deeper than just liking each other, my friend. A whole lot deeper."

"And I work for you?"

"Uh-huh. You work with me. Sometimes you work solo. And when the hammer comes down you even work for the President."

Bolan was silent for a heartbeat. "Do I get downtime?"

"What do you think?"

"We'll stay here until the cavalry arrives and see that the survivors are taken good care of. Then Riba and I are out of here. I might not have everything back in place, but I know when a piece of scum like Greg Rackham needs putting down."

"Now, that sounds like the guy I know," Brognola said. "I'll brief the incoming teams to clear you ASAP. There won't be any delays."

"With the threat Rackham is likely to be carrying with him in those vials, we can't afford *any* delays. Hal, ask the FBI to bring along a cell phone I can use."

"Will do. Do you need weapons?"

"We have ordnance. A ride back to where Riba left his truck would be handy."

"Are you sure you want to stay with this, Striker?"

"Damn sure. I don't want to think of the damage Rackham's virus could do. I just want to stop him passing it on to his customer. There's no way of knowing what *they* want to do with it."

"Understood. We're here 24/7. Anything you need, just call."

THE CDC ARRIVED FIRST, in a helicopter that disgorged hazard-suited technicians who quickly assessed the situation and took command of the lab facility. Along with Riba and Devon, Bolan was checked over thoroughly. They were all passed as hazard free. The lab was 100 percent functional, and no traces of the virus had escaped the secure section.

"We need to neutralize this area," the field supervisor told Bolan.

The doctor was a woman, dark-haired and striking. Her name tag identified her as Dr. Helen Tasker.

"How about the patients?" Bolan asked.

Med teams were inside the secure cubicles.

"The man named Bremner isn't going to make it," Tasker said. "Sorry. He's too far gone. The exterior symptoms are the least of his worries. From what my people have deduced, the virus has already started to destroy his system. Even if we counteracted it, the damage to his organs will be irreversible. I wish I could give you better news. We'll try, but I'm not happy."

"Pembury?"

"He hasn't been given such a lengthy exposure, so we might pull him through."

"No guarantees?"

"These virus permutations present us with obstacles. It's difficult to know how to treat it because we don't have the genetic blueprint to work from. When a virus is altered, it doesn't follow the normal pathways. Until we pin it down it's difficult to establish what we are working against. We'll do what we can for him."

"And this is what Rackham is hoping to sell to his client?" Riba said. "This man is sick."

"Let me see," Tasker said. "The man set this place up, developed the virus and has taken off with it in order to sell it? He doesn't seem to have any problem when it comes to out-and-out violence, and he kills if it suits his purpose. Did I miss anything? In that case, I diagnose Mr. Rackham as one really sick, amoral man."

A tight group of men pushed its way into the area. Bolan counted six of them. All were smartly dressed in suits and neat ties, wearing similar haircuts and intense expressions on their faces.

"Spooks," Tasker whispered after a cursory glance at them.

Enter the FBI, Bolan thought.

The leader of the group of agents strode up to them.

"I'm Special Agent in Charge Drake Duncan."

"In charge of what?" Tasker asked.

"This whole mess," Duncan snapped. "As of now."

Tasker turned to face him, her hands on her hips, fire in her eyes. "Fine," she said. "Shall I withdraw my team and let you boys take over? Just say so and we'll leave. The section through that door contains a lethal virus we're trying to contain, but if you want, we can pack up and go home. Just one word of caution. Lethal viruses don't respond to being ordered around, and your big guns won't scare them."

Duncan's face reddened. It was plain he didn't like to be talked down to and especially by a woman.

"My job is to control this situation…" he stated.

"Considering this *situation* was created in the first place suggests to me somewhere along the line you people weren't as on the ball as you like to make out," Tasker replied. "How the hell does someone set up an illegal facility like this anyhow?"

"By the time we got a line on it, the operation was well established."

"Oh? Agent Duncan, why doesn't that surprise me? Just stay out of my way while my people and I try to contain this mess."

She turned to Bolan. "You go and find Rackham before he sells his virus to the highest bidder." Then she turned and strode toward her team.

Duncan glanced at his own team and gave them a nod. They moved off to assess what needed to be done, leaving Bolan, Riba and Devon with the FBI SAC.

"Glad she's not mad at *me*," Riba murmured.

"She certainly speaks her mind," Duncan said. "Hell, she wasn't far wrong. We missed this, and it got away from us."

"I don't suppose Rackham did a deal to advertise what he was doing," Bolan said.

Duncan rubbed his hand across his face and took a breath. "You're Cooper?"

Bolan nodded and held out a hand. The FBI agent took it.

"Bremner—I'm sorry for what's happened to him," Bolan stated.

"Bremner. And Kim. Not my best week."

"How is Kim?"

"He'll be okay. They fixed his shoulder. It'll keep him off work a few months." Duncan cleared his throat. "I owe you my thanks for getting him medical help when you did. It made a difference."

"It was unfortunate that I walked in when I did," Bolan said. "I was tracking Callum and caught up just when Kim was completing his meet."

"You weren't in the loop, so how could you know? What the hell, Cooper, this isn't the first time it's happened. Covert operations are what they are, so screwups happen. At least we got our hands on the virus sample and Callum cuffed to a hospital bed."

"Has he given up any helpful information yet?"

Duncan shook his head. "Nothing. I think he's trying to work out how to make a deal."

"I could try some old-fashioned Apache persuasion," Riba said.

"After realizing what these people have been doing," Duncan said, "I wish I could oblige." He clenched his fists in sheer frustration. "They were doing it for money. Nothing else but money. That's what pisses me off. Not for some mistaken political beliefs. Not for misplaced patriotism. But *money.*"

"How far did Bremner get into Rackham's setup?" Bolan asked. "Is he working alone, or is he part of some criminal organization?"

"That's the hell of it. He'd reported he was getting close to finding out. He disappeared before he had the chance to update us on this place."

"You knew him well?"

"Yeah. Years. He was a damn good agent. A good team player and a good undercover agent. He'd worked a number of sting operations successfully. He had the ability to take on a new persona so damned easily. Sometimes he'd vanish for weeks, then come up with the goods so we could move in." Duncan paused. "I'll miss him."

"Is he a family man?"

"Thankfully no. Apart from a sister who lives in Hawaii. I'll tell her myself. I gave him the assignment, so it's down to me."

One of Duncan's agents approached and spoke quietly to the man. After he had moved on, Duncan turned back to Bolan. He reached into his jacket and withdrew a cell phone. He passed it across.

"I was asked to deliver this by my section chief. It's fully charged." Duncan smiled. "I was asked—*told*—not to ask too many questions where you are concerned. It appears you have the ear of the President, no less. From what my chief said, you have anonymity stamped all over you."

Bolan took the cell. "Thanks. As for the rest, it's the nature of my work. I don't have any ties to known agencies, but I'm not in competition with any of them. I have the greatest respect for all of you."

Duncan had taken a long look at Bolan's appearance. "Looks as if you've been busy out there. Anything we need to know?"

"Some bodies in the forest," Bolan said. "They were determined to prevent us reaching the facility. And while we were doing that, Rackham slipped away. No doubt to arrange final delivery of his virus."

"My people will be making a search. Let's hope we can come up with results sooner rather than later."

"I'm sure you and your people can deal with things here," Bolan said. "Riba and I need to move ourselves. First we need to deliver a certain young lady back home. It's time she was relieved from duty."

"She isn't part of your team?"

"No. Just an innocent who got caught up in things and stayed on board to offer help. I'm relieved she came through without serious injury."

"You'll find my number in the cell's directory," Duncan said to Bolan. "Call if you have any information, or need me."

Riba indicated Bolan's clothing. "He could do with the name of your tailor."

"Duncan, we need a ride to backtrack and pick up Riba's truck and Laura's wheels," Bolan said.

"No problem." Duncan called over one of his men and told him to give Bolan and Riba a ride. As they followed the agent out, picking up Devon from where she was waiting, Duncan said, "Find him, Cooper. Do what you have to. Just find him."

"Consider it done," Bolan said.

Duncan recognized something in the man's voice that confirmed there would be no backing off from that promise.

"Okay," he said to himself. "Time to go and make peace with Dr. Tasker."

16

"Did you trust Duncan?" Devon asked. She was in the rear seat of Riba's truck as he picked up the route she had described for him. "I'm not sure I did."

"Very cynical," Riba commented. "You've been around Cooper too much."

"You think?"

"Duncan is FBI," Bolan said. "They exist in a closed world. It rubs off so they come across as not trusting anyone. The man has a difficult job to do."

"You're not exactly in the fun business."

"No, but my winning personality helps me through."

Bolan had been silent for a long time, staring out through the rain-streaked windshield. His mind was grappling with facts concerning the current situation as well as filtering through the foggy pieces of jumbled memories.

"Hey," Devon said, resting a hand on his shoulder. "Are things coming back?"

He nodded briefly. "Names. Some places. The memories are fragmented and hard to slot into place."

"Don't fight them," Devon said. "Let them come back on their own."

"You remember you still owe me that hundred dollars?" Riba said.

"No."

Riba grunted. "Yeah, he's getting better," he said, grinning into the rearview mirror for Devon's benefit. "We'll miss you."

The woman slumped back in her seat. "You're dumping me again," she said. "Leaving me back at the diner."

"It's time you got back to your normal life," Bolan said gently. "I won't put you in any more risk. And this time you stay put."

"I get the message. You've had to pull *me* out of trouble once too often."

"Think yourself lucky you can quit while you're ahead," Riba said. "I figure Cooper and me are going to need to head after Rackham. And it's no place for a nice young lady where we'll be going."

Bolan twisted in his seat to catch her attention. "One thing, Laura…"

"I know. Don't mention anything about what Rackham plans. No talk about missing viruses."

Bolan nodded, knowing he didn't need to worry on that score.

"Joshua, let's go pick up the lady's wheels."

THE DINER WAS A WELCOME sight as Riba rolled into the parking lot, Devon following closely behind in her Jeep. As they climbed out of the truck, the door opened and Mitchell appeared. The relief was plain to see on his face as he watched Devon park her Jeep and join them.

"I was starting to worry," he said.

"No need," Devon said. "I had protection."

She hugged Mitchell. He stared at her disheveled appearance.

The diner was deserted, but the smell of brewing coffee reached them. Mitchell led the way. "Sam's been hopping mad 'cause he can't get any details."

"Truthfully, Vern, he doesn't need to hear any details."

Mitchell glanced at Bolan. "Like that, huh?"

"Laura's back. He'll have to be satisfied with that."

"I need to tidy up," the woman said as she left them.

The lingering look she offered Bolan told him she understood he needed to move on.

"She going to be okay?"

"That's one great girl," Riba replied. "I think she'll be fine."

"Tell her we had to go," Bolan said. "No more time left. She knows why."

BACK ON THE ROAD BOLAN said, "You got a clean shirt back there in your gear?"

Riba looked him up and down. "I was wondering when you might ask. Go help yourself. I always carry changes of clothing when I'm working. It should fit you pretty well. We're about the same size."

Bolan slid into the rear of the cab. He located a dark shirt and a pair of pants.

"You having any more flashbacks?"

"Names without faces. A couple of faces but no names."

"How's the headache?"

"Easing, but it's not going to go away so easily. As soon as I start making myself try to remember, it returns."

"You should come back home with me. Spend some time in the sweat lodge. Good place to meditate. It gives the body and mind a chance to get purification. No joke, it works. All that hot steam drives out the bad spirits and lets good thoughts in."

Bolan climbed back into the passenger seat. "Joshua, I might take you up on that."

Riba gave a noncommittal grunt. "This might seem like a weird question, but just where are we heading?"

"The hospital where Callum is being looked after. He needs to answer a couple of questions."

Bolan took out his cell phone and called Brognola. He explained what he needed and was promised a swift return call. The call came much quicker than Bolan had expected.

"You always this fast?"

"We try to be. I got your location. I understand the urgency, so I called ahead after I spoke to your new best bud Duncan. You have the okay to question Callum."

"I'll keep you updated."

Bolan relayed the hospital location to Riba. He keyed it into the truck's navigation system.

"It should take us just around forty minutes." When Bolan didn't reply Riba said, "What?"

"What if Rackham decides Callum has outlived his usefulness? That he presents a high risk factor if he stays alive?"

"You think he might try for him at the hospital? Cooper, that would be crazy. Rackham would have to know Callum will be under close protection."

"The man doesn't play by normal rules, Joshua. Whoever's behind him seem to have plenty of funds to hire whatever they need. They might decide it's worth the risk to silence Callum before he decides to talk. I better contact Duncan."

"This just gets better," Riba said. "Shut down one part and something else takes its place."

"WE HAVE A THREE-MAN team watching over him," Duncan said after a perfunctory greeting to Bolan. "I'll see if I can pull in a few more. The trouble is, we're a little thin on the ground around here. I can do it, but it might take time."

"We're close," Bolan said. "We'll rack up the speed and hope the local P.D. isn't around. I'll keep you updated, Duncan."

17

"What do you think?" Riba asked. "Looks peaceful enough to me."

They had pulled into the quiet lot in front of the hospital. Bolan scanned the area. About thirty cars were parked around them. He looked beyond the parking lot to the highway nearby. Nothing seemed out of place. It was just a normal neighborhood going about its business. Traffic was light due to the rain.

"Let's do this," he said. "The longer we wait the more chance trouble could show."

They climbed out of the SUV and ran across the lot to the hospital entrance.

"Do you think it ever stops raining in this damn place?" Riba grumbled, slapping his hat against his leg.

"Let's hope we don't need to stay long enough to find out."

They stepped inside as the automatic doors slid open. The reception area was quiet. A couple of uniformed hospital staff stood behind the curved desk, and a smartly dressed young man seated on one of the chairs ranged along one side of the area. He pushed to feet as Bolan and Riba appeared.

"He's got to be FBI," Riba said. "He's dressed so neat and tidy."

"Mr. Cooper? Mr. Riba? I'm Agent Travis. I was told to expect you by…"

"Agent Duncan?" Bolan said.

Travis nodded. "I'll take you up to Mr. Callum."

"How is he?"

"Medically fine. The bullet was removed and Mr. Callum has been made comfortable."

"So he's okay?" Riba said.

"He keeps threatening everyone. To be honest, the man is a pain. It's hard to feel any sympathy for him."

"Have you been told what he tried to do?" Bolan asked, and when Travis nodded, Bolan said, "Then he's lost the right for sympathy."

They took an elevator to the next floor. Private rooms stretched the length of the open corridor. To their left the glass front wall extended up from below in a continuous curve, providing the maximum amount of daylight. Travis led them to a door that had another FBI agent standing watch.

"We have one more man inside," Travis explained. "SAC Duncan is trying to get some more people to help out."

He pushed through the door and led the way into the room.

Callum was propped up on the bed, his shoulder swathed in bandages. His free hand was cuffed to the headboard. When he recognized Bolan, his anger burst to the surface.

"He's the one who shot me. Came crashing in on me and shot me."

"If I have the facts correct, Callum, *you* shot an undercover agent while you were in the act of supplying a deadly virus."

"Yeah? He knew the game he was playing."

"You think that excuses you?" Bolan said.

"I was tricked."

"Your intentions contravened Code 18," Travis said. "Which means you are still guilty."

Callum's anger caused him to surge forward, pulling at the drip tubes feeding into his arm. "Don't quote your goddamn rules at me."

Bolan said, "I'd take note, Callum. Code 18 has become very important in your life. If it goes against you in court, you get the death penalty. I'd think about that. No jail time where you finally might get out. Code 18 delivers a short walk to the execution chamber. End of the line. Is that worth whatever Rackham was paying you?"

Travis glanced sideways at Bolan, studying the taut profile of this man who had been allowed to question the prisoner. He hadn't inquired why Cooper had been allowed the privilege. It wasn't his right to ask why. Duncan was his superior. It was his call. Travis was simply curious.

"I'm wondering," Bolan said. "Who runs your organization? Not Rackham. He's just the local gofer, taking orders from someone else."

"What makes you say that?" Travis asked.

"Look at Callum. He's way down the ladder. A plain and simple grunt, doing the dirty work and getting hung out to dry."

"Hey, I'm still here," Callum said.

Travis ignored him, having picked up Bolan's ploy.

"I hear Rackham has moved on. Left the facility now that he's got what he needs."

"He'll do his deal and take the money."

"Leaving Callum to take the flak."

"Smart move. While we concentrate on the facility and Callum, Rackham walks free and clear."

"Got to hand it to the man."

"You figure all this cross talk is going to get me to give you information?"

Bolan glanced at him, smiling. "Callum, if you figure protecting Rackham is going to save your ass, think again. He doesn't need you. The facility is down. FBI and CDC are all over it. Your buddies are dead or in handcuffs. Rackham has his goods, and he's going to sell them. End of the line. No one is coming to bail you out."

"On the other hand, you might have callers. I'd guess any visitors you get from Rackham will be on line to make sure you *don't* talk," Travis said. "The man is going to be tying up loose ends."

Callum's gaze alternated between Bolan and Travis. He even glanced in Riba's direction. The P.I. returned his scrutiny with stoic indifference.

"Rackham wouldn't do that," Callum said. "We've known each other for a long time."

"In that case," Travis said, "I can pull my detail and send them away. No point wasting taxpayer money if they're not needed. Hospital security can take over."

"You're leaving me with bloody rent-a-cops?"

"They'll handle things until you can be moved," Travis said.

"Moved to the morgue," Callum muttered, suddenly beginning to feel exposed.

"Callum," Bolan said, "if you want protection, offer us something to work with."

"You're not getting out of here," Travis added. "Understand that right now. Make a plea to lessen your sentence by giving us some help. I'll make sure my boss gets to hear about it. But if you want to play hardball, see what *that* gets you. It's a limited offer. If one of your buddies back at the facility talks first, the offer is off the table. He'll plea bargain and you get nothing."

"How do I know you won't screw me? Suppose I did give you information. How do I guarantee protection?"

"Weigh the odds," Bolan said. "Trust us, or cling to the hope Rackham comes through for you. Make your choice."

"If I talk, I could disappear once you get what you want."

Travis conveyed dismay. "Are you suggesting the FBI would allow that to happen to a witness?"

Callum shook his head, turning to Bolan. "Is this junior G-man for real? Hasn't he heard about people going missing?"

"I'd trust him," Bolan said. "He's your best chance out of a poor choice."

"Easy for you to say. If Rackham learns I pointed the finger, he's going to want me dead."

"No need for him to learn who pointed the finger," Travis said. "Just give us a location. We'll act on it and nothing will be traced back to you."

"As long as Rackham is alive, he'll find out."

Bolan moved closer to the bed. "Only if he stays alive, which is unlikely," he said, so quietly Travis failed to pick up his words.

Callum met Bolan's unflinching stare. He understood what the big man had said. The inference was clear.

The man was openly promising Rackham wouldn't walk away when it was all over.

"I want immunity from prosecution," Callum demanded. "I give you Rackham, I walk free."

Bolan glanced at Travis and saw the FBI agent turn aside and cross the room, taking out his cell phone. He spoke into it quietly for a few moments. Callum was watching him with a look of desperation in his eyes; he understood his position and was playing the only card he had left.

Travis ended his call. He dropped his cell phone back in his pocket and faced Callum. "This is the deal. You give us Rackham. Tell us where we can find him. If it works out and we take him down, you go free. No result, no deal."

"That's what I call a crap hand," Callum said bitterly.

"Callum, it's more than you deserve," Bolan said. "Figure yourself lucky."

"You call this lucky?"

Bolan's smile was ice-cold. "Oh, yes. Lucky because you're making your deal with the FBI and not me."

"You hear what he said?" Callum yelled. "That son of a bitch will kill me if he gets the chance."

"Then let's talk before I walk out of here and give him the opportunity," Travis said.

Callum saw he was getting no consideration from the FBI

agent. His options were limited as to be nonexistent. If he was to come through this with a chance, however slim, he was going to need to cooperate.

"Rackham will be at the backup location. Up near the Canadian border. That's where he'll have fixed the meet with his Korean clients."

"You know where it is?" Travis asked.

"I've been there once. I can give you its location."

Callum indicated his belongings in a plastic bag on the locker next to his bed. "My cell. The GPS coordinates are logged in."

Riba took the bag and unsealed it. He took out the cell phone and switched it on. He handed it to Callum and stood close to the bed as the man scrolled through the menu. Callum handed the cell phone back to Riba.

"GPS coordinates," the P.I. said. "Looks like we're in business." He handed the device to Bolan.

"Anything we need to know?" Bolan asked Callum.

"Only that there's a small airstrip near the house. That's all I got."

"Travis, you'd better call Duncan," Bolan said. "He's short on additional backup. Tell him we're heading for the location. I promised him I wouldn't let Rackham slip away. I'll keep that promise. And I can move faster without all the official maneuvering you people have to go through."

Travis followed Bolan and Riba as they left the room.

"Cooper, I need that location in case we *can* get a team on the move."

Bolan showed him the cell phone and Travis copied down the coordinates.

"Rackham might have backup with him," the FBI agent said. "Shouldn't you wait for reinforcements?"

"Rackham isn't going to stay around once he does his deal. We may already be running late."

Travis watched Bolan and Riba walk away. He thought about the virus and the harm it could do if it was released.

"Then let's hope you're not too late," he said.

18

"We're are cutting this close," Riba said. "Awful close, part-ner."

"Don't remind me."

"When this is done, you need big R & R. Time to get your head clear."

"Crazy as it sounds, that's already happening."

"Memories?"

"Some. Coming in from the past. Names. Places. Still hazy but a damn sight better than having no recollection."

"Nothing recent?"

"Fragments. Brognola a little more. A guy called Grimaldi. He's a pilot. We go back a long way."

"What about the headaches?"

"Eased some."

Bolan's cell phone rang. It was Duncan.

"Just an update," the FBI SAC said. "The facility is now in complete lockdown. Our good Dr. Tasker has isolated the lab and Pembury has been stabilized."

"Is he going to survive?"

"The prognosis is hopeful."

"What about his wife?"

"We have an operation in progress to rescue her," Duncan said. "Pembury has been cooperating as much as he's able. Travis tells me you're en route to Rackham's location. I've managed to get satellite surveillance on those coordinates.

We have a real-time image that I'm looking at. It shows the building, which appears to be a large lodge. There are vehicles parked out front, and an airstrip to the rear shows a helicopter landed no more than fifteen minutes ago."

"Can you run a check on the registration numbers? It could help."

"I'm attempting that as we speak. No luck at the moment. The satellite can't get a decent angle on the fuselage. We'll keep trying."

"We need another forty minutes to reach the place," Bolan said, checking the navigation unit where they had tapped in the GPS coordinates. "If that bird leaves before we get there, you'll need to track and intercept when it lands, or before."

"Will do. Let's hope you can get there first. There's no way I want any local interference at this stage, but if we see the need I might have to call in the local law. If they're seen, Rackham might make a reckless move. I don't want that virus being used as an offensive weapon to save his own ass. Rackham has shown what a heartless bastard he is. There's no telling what he might do if he's cornered."

"Rackham won't quit without a fight."

The FBI agent sighed. "This gets better every time I turn around."

"You make it your priority to stop that helicopter if it gets off the ground. Call in the Air Force to burn it out of the sky if it does."

"Hope it doesn't come to that."

"Hard choices, Duncan. They come with the territory."

"Thanks for reminding me, Cooper."

"Keep us updated," Bolan said. He ended the call and contacted Brognola.

"How's it going, Striker?"

Bolan gave him an update on the situation. "If we can reach Rackham before his buyer takes off, we can end it fast. Isolate the virus and wait for the CDC to show up."

"We homed in on this Greg Rackham. Former special ops. The guy branched out into private security when his time was up. He ran his own operation for a few years, recruiting some old military buddies. He provided personal protection. Worked off the books for a number of dubious people. Then his operations kind of went dark for a year. It appears he linked up with some other group we can't get much information on. Our checks into his current associations keep getting blocked. At a guess I'd have to say Rackham has some powerful backers who don't welcome being investigated."

"Agency connections? OrgCrime?"

"Hard getting any definite line on them at the moment, but we'll keep looking."

"That won't sit well with Bear. He doesn't like striking out," Bolan said. He realized then what he had said. "That came out of nowhere."

"You remember him?"

"In a wheelchair. Top man running intelligence gathering."

"Well, he'll love you for giving him that title," Brognola said.

He didn't press Bolan for any more information. He was just pleased the guy was starting to remember things.

"Duncan has Rackham's location under satellite surveillance. I suggested he call in Air Force help if that chopper does take off before we show."

"Good call. How's Riba doing?"

"Right now he's making a fair chauffeur. I might keep him on after this."

"Any more talk like that and I'll make you get out and walk," Riba said.

The road ahead began to wind through densely timbered terrain. The ranked trees closed in on them. The sky to the north was thickly clouded, but the rain held off for the moment.

Bolan used the time to relax, pleased that the turbulence

in his skull had subsided to a level he could tolerate. He left Riba to navigate.

He watched the road. The image was soothing and Bolan allowed his gaze to wander, the unwinding scenery lulling him. With all that had been happening over the past few days, these moments of relative calm were welcome. He let it happen. When they reached their destination it would all change.

Greg Rackham would resist. That was a sure thing. The man was dedicated to his cause, whatever lay behind it. He would utilize his people, and there would be no hesitation if it came to killing.

LISE DELAWARE MADE CERTAIN she was alone before she made the call on her cell phone. She listened to the number ring. The distant phone was picked up. No one spoke until Delaware identified herself.

"I hope this is better news than previously," a man's voice said.

"We're within a short time of completing the deal," Delaware reported. "Rackham is with the Koreans now. They're negotiating terms. I believe he'll make a good deal."

"He needs to, following the disasters of the past few days. We haven't been impressed by his handling of matters. Mistakes like the ones we have seen can severely affect our reputation."

"Rackham is well aware of his failings. But if he completes the deal, I think he'll have gone a long way to regain our favor."

"The matter rests with you, Lise. Any final decisions you make will be accepted."

"Good to hear."

"What about the Korean who broke up the first deal?"

"A ringer. It looks like he removed the genuine North Korean operative and took his place. His game might have worked if this Cooper guy hadn't stepped in and blown the whole thing apart."

"Who is this man, Lise? From what you've been reporting he's caused some problems for you all."

"There's no denying that. The man has proved to be a damned nuisance. And hard to remove. I've had our people running checks on him from every direction. We aren't having any luck. Every lead we follow comes to a dead stop. No affiliations with any known agencies. He comes and goes like a damned shadow. I'd be lying if I said it was going to be easy dealing with him. The man is good. I need a few like him on our payroll."

"Keep trying. You have me intrigued now. A man like this could prove a real problem to us. If he is as skilled as you say, then we need to contain him if we can. When this Korean deal is completed, you have our permission to look into this man's background. Do what you have to."

"And Rackham?"

"His future is in the balance. Let's see how he handles the rest of the deal before we make any final decisions. I understand you have feelings for him, Lise, but his recent performance leaves a lot to desire."

"I understand. Let me assess the situation. I'll come back to you."

Delaware broke the connection. She stood at the window and stared out across the rain-swept grounds surrounding the house.

Her curiosity had been roused by Cooper. He was skilled at what he did. She knew what had happened to him recently, yet he still had managed to overcome everything thrown his way. Hurt both physically and mentally, he had kept pursuing his goals. His persistence got to her, and she found she was attracted to the man. He made Greg Rackham look like an underachiever. Taking Cooper on would be a challenge she could look forward to. If they both survived the current clash, Lise Delaware would anticipate future involvement with the man, in whatever form it took.

19

Riba pulled into a stand of trees and cut the engine. The navigation system had brought them to within a half mile of the location. They had decided to walk in the final stretch in case Rackham had posted sentries.

They made their final weapon checks and left the SUV behind as they moved into the cover of the trees and undergrowth.

The ground was reasonably level underfoot. The thick carpet of the forest floor was still sodden from the falling rain, and they made no sound as they approached the distant lodge. Bolan let Riba take point. The man was at home in a situation like this. His senses allowed him to assess what lay around them. Bolan realized the advantages of having a full-blooded Apache as a partner at this particular moment.

Closer in, Riba held up a hand, gesturing for Bolan to take cover.

He had spotted movement ahead.

A single sentry carried an SMG. The guy was scanning the area, but he lacked the skill that would make him a threat to Riba.

Laying down his own weapon, Riba drew his knife and moved forward silently, slipping out of sight through the undergrowth. Bolan lost sight of his partner. He spotted the sentry, staring about him, then glimpsed a dark shape rising behind the man. There was a brief flurry of movement with very little sound. The sentry went down. Moments later Riba came into view, gesturing for Bolan to join him.

The soldier retrieved his partner's weapon, handing it to the man when he reached him.

"These idiots almost make it too damned easy," Riba said.

"There could be others."

"Over on the far side where the landing strip is. There's likely to be somebody there."

"I'll handle the lodge," Bolan said. "How about you go and make sure that chopper can't take off."

"Suits me."

"Could be more than one back there. Sentries. Maybe the plane's crew. You okay with that?" Bolan asked his partner.

"If I get to shoot things up," Riba said, "how would I not be okay?"

Bolan smiled, said, "As soon as you hear firing, it's your signal to go. That chopper doesn't leave the ground."

Riba nodded and loped off into the undergrowth, making a run for the landing strip and the waiting helicopter.

The moment the man was out of sight, Bolan started for the house. Rackham was inside, cutting his deal. The moment an agreement was reached, the Koreans would be leaving, along with their purchase.

Mack Bolan was going to cancel the deal and take down those involved. If he achieved nothing else this day, Greg Rackham wasn't going to hand over the virus. The man's intention was clear. He would sell the vials containing the deadly virus to his buyer and walk away with a fortune for his organization. Wholesale slaughter could ensue. There would be suffering and death for thousands. A country plunged into horror as the effects of the virulent plague ravaged it. Bolan wouldn't let that happen.

Skirting the shrubbery, the soldier crouched, scanning the way ahead. The parked vehicles offered him cover for the next stage of his assault. The vehicles were the final obstacle before he reached the main entrance. Bolan checked his position and the presence of exterior guards.

Three of them stood around the parked cars. They were all armed. Two had P90s. The third was the only one who appeared to be alert. Bolan knew that would make no difference. Sentences had already been passed. The Executioner was here to carry them out.

He ran a final check, making certain his own weapon was ready, then eased around the rear of the closest SUV. Bolan raised himself from cover long enough to shoulder the P90. His finger stroked the trigger, sending a burst of 5.7 mm slugs into the back of his target's skull, the impacts driving the guy's head forward. Blood and bone erupted from the wounds. Even as the guy started to drop, Bolan swung the P90 in a short arc, firing on the move. Hot slugs cored into the other two guards as they reached for their weapons. They both took chest shots, bodies twisting as they were hit.

Bolan broke cover, making for the front of the sprawling building. He flattened against the wall to the left of the wide entrance as an eruption of raised voices reached him. A pair of armed men spilled out of the doorway, saw the downed trio of sentries and hauled themselves to a stop. Bolan caught them in his sights and laid devastating bursts into their exposed bodies, driving them to the ground with misty spurts of blood jetting from their chests.

Turning, Bolan went in through the doorway, emerging in the wide entrance hall. He swung the P90 left and right, searching for targets. As raised voices sounded from his far left, Bolan heard the beat of footsteps.

The armed men who burst into sight were Asian. They were yelling wildly, using the force of their voices as intimidating threats. The sounds didn't disturb Bolan. He was more concerned with the bulky SMGs the gunners wielded.

One opened up, the heavy clatter of noise drowning out the

yells of the men. Slugs peppered the wall and floor, chips of plaster erupting into the air and showering Bolan.

The Executioner had already dropped to the floor, rolling to one side. He turned on his stomach, thrusting the P90 into position. He scythed the weapon in a deadly sweep, the 5.7 mm slugs cutting into limbs and lower torsos. Blood spurted as the projectiles cut through flesh and bone, dropping the men to the floor. Bolan pushed upright, moving forward, and delivered head shots that stilled the writhing figures.

He walked on, seeking his prime targets.

The buyers.

The backup.

And Greg Rackham.

20

Prior to Bolan breaching the house, Riba had reached *his* target, working his way in a half circle until he was concealed by the bulk of a maintenance hut.

A Bell 429 helicopter stood on the strip, rotors turning over on idle. The passenger-side hatch was open, and a pair of armed Koreans were positioned at the access door, on standby.

They hadn't spotted Riba. He was still covered by the maintenance hut standing back from the strip. He watched and waited, in no hurry to engage. The P.I. was waiting for Bolan to make his move. He didn't have to wait long.

The distant crackle of autofire came from the direction of the house. The Korean guards glanced at each other, unsure what to do, until Riba made up their minds for them.

When he broke cover, moving swiftly for his size, Riba's P90 was up and firing. By the time the guards realized *they* were under attack, Riba had his targets.

He put the closer guy down with a long burst from the P90. The Korean stumbled and went down hard on the strip. His partner returned fire, his shots coming close but not close enough to hit Riba. The P.I. hauled himself to a dead stop, tracked in with his SMG and hit the surviving guard with a long burst that shredded his torso, climbing to core in and tear at his heart. The guy toppled back against the helicopter's fuselage, leaving a bloody smear as he slid along the smooth surface and collapsed.

Riba heard the turbines start to whine as the pilot increased the engine's power, deciding it was no longer safe to wait around. Riba closed in on the chopper, aiming his SMG at the tail rotor. The burst of slugs chewed at the spring blades and took them apart. Raising the muzzle, the P.I. emptied his magazine into the engine casing, the slugs puncturing the aluminum and burrowing into the engine itself. The power plant wound down, smoke starting to stream from the rear of the compartment.

Standing back, Riba ejected his spent magazine and eased in a fresh one.

He caught movement behind the cockpit canopy. A side window slid open and a man leaned out. He held a pistol in his hand and started to fire in Riba's direction, the ill-judged shots cracking against the tarmac.

"Want to play?" Riba muttered.

He swung the P90 up and triggered a burst at the cockpit canopy. The canopy shattered as the shots ripped into the cabin. Over the crackle of slugs he heard a pained yell. The pistol slipped from the shooter's hand and his arm dropped to hang loosely from the opening.

Flame had started to flare from the engine housing. Thoughts of tanks full of aviation fuel reminded Riba to back off. He was walking away when he heard the dull thump of an explosion behind him. He didn't look back to see flames curling out from the engine cowling, content that the Bell wouldn't be going anywhere.

Nor would its Korean crew.

Or its passengers.

BOLAN'S MOVE WAS OVERLAID by silence.

No sound.

No movement.

He took that as a threat and reacted accordingly. He eased in against the wall, the opening some fifteen feet ahead. If anyone was waiting for him, he wasn't going to present an easy target. The square of light spilling out from the room was unbroken, no shadows telling him where its occupants might be standing.

He had no idea how many were waiting for him, how many were armed.

He doubted Rackham would be unarmed.

Or his Korean buyers.

How many guards did the Koreans and Rackham have with them?

Bolan's head buzzed with all the thoughts he was juggling. He felt as if he was working up to an overload. Too much all at once. He pushed all thoughts to the recesses of his mind, concentrating on the present. The problem was that other matters persisted. They refused to stay dormant. They were demanding his attention.

Names.

Places.

Jostling for his time.

It was the *wrong* time. It shouldn't be happening now. He needed to concentrate on what was waiting for him inside that room.

Sweat glistened on Bolan's face. He gripped the P90 as he closed on the bright outline of the opening, pausing long enough to check his rear. Nothing. Only the dead sprawled on the bloodstained floor.

He picked up the merest whisper of sound from the opening: the rustle of clothing, a flicker of shadow in the oblong box of light spilling out across the floor. A distorted image paused, then drew back. Then he heard a voice.

Only a whisper.

The voice rose, became almost a shout.

It was sharp, commanding and female.

Bolan had no memory of a woman at the facility.

So who was she?

He didn't allow it to distract his attention. It was unimportant for the moment. His overriding concern was for the virus Rackham was hoping to trade with the Koreans. That above everything was his target. Rackham was intent on completing his negotiating. If he succeeded and the virus was taken out of the country…

A harsh command rang out in Korean. A second voice responded.

Bolan heard the rush of footsteps. A shadow extended across the floor, growing larger as it approached the opening.

A figure burst into view. The guy had a pistol in one hand, and he launched himself in a forward roll that spun him across the passage. The guy recovered quickly, the brandished pistol seeking a target. And the guy was fast. He located Bolan in seconds, his broad face fixed in a hard scowl as he triggered his weapon, the heavy-caliber pistol slamming out multiple shots that blasted chunks of plaster from the wall inches from their intended target; if the man had been allowed a few seconds to settle his aim, he might have succeeded in hitting Bolan.

The Executioner sank to a semicrouch, the muzzle of the P90 gaining advantage over the moving Korean and delivering its powerful burst on target. The Korean gave a harsh scream as he felt the bite of multiple 5.7 mm slugs burning into his body. He tumbled away from Bolan, the final shot from his pistol burying itself in the high ceiling.

Voices reached Bolan from inside the room. He took a moment to set himself, then moved to the far side of the opening, knowing he was briefly exposing himself. He ducked into cover as a weapon fired from inside the room, the single slug ripping a sliver of wood from the edge of the doorframe.

He was able to see farther into the room from his new position. A cluster of figures faced the opening.

Rackham stood beside a low table, a black case set in front of him.

A pair of Koreans flanked the man, one wielding an SMG. Behind Rackham, to one side, a lean American held a SPAS combat shotgun.

And at one end of the table was a tall, dark-clad woman. A trimmed cap of black hair framed a face that could have been described as beautiful, except it was marred by a harsh expression that formed an angry mask. Her eyes, fixed on Bolan, held a gleam of utter contempt as she pulled a Desert Eagle pistol from under the leather jacket she wore. Bolan noticed, almost as an abstract, that she wore thin black leather gloves.

From the look in her eyes, Bolan knew there would be no hesitation once she had her weapon on line.

He triggered the P90, spraying the room and the enemy as he went through the opening, feeling the chatter of the weapon as it fired. His full-on assault caught the room's occupants wanting. His initial burst found the Koreans, their faces registering shock as the 5.7 mm slugs hit, smashing into them chest-high and pushing them away from the table. The guy behind Rackham reached out to shove his superior away from the line of fire, swinging up the hefty-looking SPAS combat shotgun he held. He fired a couple of seconds too fast, the powerful spread of shot missing Bolan by feet. He dropped, bringing his P90 on line, and hit the shotgunner with a short burst that tore the guy's throat out.

Straightening, Bolan tracked Rackham and the woman.

She swiveled at the waist, the heavy Magnum Desert Eagle comfortable in her hand as she brought the muzzle round. The big pistol thundered loudly in the room. Bolan felt the hot wind of the .357 slug as it fanned his cheek.

The moment she fired, the woman stepped to one side, away from the table. As she went she fired again and the heavy slug clipped Bolan's sleeve.

Out the corner of his eye Bolan saw Rackham leaning forward, his own SMG snatched up from the table, the muzzle seeking a target. Rackham opened fire, his burst cleaving the air where Bolan had been standing a split second before he had moved.

The soldier returned fire.

He hit Rackham in the lower torso with a long burst, the slugs coring in and severing the man's spine as they blew out through his back. Rackham screamed as his shattered spine cut the life from his limbs. He toppled forward across the table, his flailing arms sweeping its surface. He slammed facedown on the table, blood flowering as his nose was crushed.

The big Desert Eagle boomed as the black-clad woman fired again. Twice. Her shots forced Bolan to pull aside, giving her a few seconds to make a grab for the case still on the table. She caught hold of it in her left hand, pulling it with her as she fired again in Bolan's direction before making a direct run for the window.

The Executioner pushed upright, bringing his SMG on line, the muzzle lining up.

The woman had covered her face with her right arm as she hit the glass. It shattered as she burst through, long legs powering her forward.

Bolan's finger stroked the trigger. The P90 fired a few remaining shots before it locked on empty.

The dark-clad figure twisted to one side as a single slug clipped her left arm. Her grip on the case slackened and it fell free, hitting the frame of the window and dropping back inside the room.

Then she was gone, in a shower of glass fragments, landing outside. It seemed she was about to fall, but with a supreme effort she righted herself and vanished from sight.

By the time Bolan reached the window she was almost out of sight, dodging athletically between the parked cars. He would have followed, but his attention was drawn to the black case she had dropped. That was his priority. He picked it up and carried it to the middle of the room before he set it down.

Bolan crossed the room, kicking weapons clear of bodies to prevent anyone still alive from attempting to retrieve them.

He looked back at the case. He saw it was the same design as the one recovered from Callum in the hotel room. It had been dropped only a couple of feet and looked intact. Bolan considered opening it, but decided that would be a foolish move. He would leave that for the CDC experts.

The sound of an engine reached his ears. Tires whined as a vehicle pulled away at a fast rate. Peering through the window, Bolan caught a glimpse of a big SUV speeding out the gate.

The woman.

It had to be.

She was getting away. She was leaving without the virus.

Bolan heard someone moaning. The sound came from Greg Rackham. He was lying half-across the table and raised his head when Bolan approached. Blood dribbled from his slack mouth, and Bolan could see more spreading out from under his body.

"I can't move," he whispered. "You tore out my spine, you bastard. I'm crippled."

"You expecting sympathy?"

"Look at me, Cooper. Look what you did to me."

"I'm looking and what I see is a piece of garbage who infected humans with a killer virus just to make sure it worked."

"It was a business decision."

"Right now do you think it was worth it?"

Bolan took out his cell phone and keyed in Duncan's number.

"Cooper?"

"It's done," Bolan said. "I have the virus. Get the CDC here fast because I don't know if the samples have been damaged and I'm not opening the case to check."

"Cooper. Did you get them all?"

"Except Rackham's female accomplice. She took a car and ran. But she left the virus behind."

"Are they all dead?"

Bolan stared into Rackham's empty eyes. "Almost."

He shut down the cell phone and took out the SIG Sauer pistol, prepared to deliver a mercy round.

"Do it," Rackham whispered.

"Answer a couple of questions first."

JOSHUA RIBA MADE HIS way into the house, following the trail of the dead. He was feet away from the room when a single shot sent echoes along the passage.

"Cooper?"

"In here," Bolan said.

Riba scanned the room, saw the bodies, the streaks of blood and the empty bullet casings.

"The chopper won't fly," Riba said. "Problems with the engine."

"I heard," Bolan said. He indicated the case on the floor in the center of the room. "The virus is in there. CDC is on its way."

Riba spotted Rackham's body stretched across the low table. The back of his head had been blown open by a single bullet.

"Call it a mercy shot," Bolan said. "His spine was shattered. He wasn't about to move by himself again."

"You are too soft, Cooper," Riba said. "What he did to those people he deserved to suffer."

"We made a bargain," Bolan said, his voice sounding suddenly weary. "He answered my questions and I gave him what he wanted."

"What questions?"

"You hear a car move off?"

Riba nodded.

"His female accomplice. She tried to take the virus with her when she went through the window. Lucky for us she dropped it. I asked Rackham who she was. Her name is Lise

Delaware. She and Rackham worked for a criminal organization called HEGRE."

"I never heard of it," Riba said.

"I didn't until now. But Rackham said it's an organized group that operates globally. Powerful and ruthless. HEGRE set up the facility and put Rackham in charge, with the woman as his second in command. According to Rackham, they'll operate anywhere, take on any criminal activity if it pays off. They have connections in big business. And in governments. From what he said, HEGRE doesn't take interference very well."

Riba ran a hand through his thick black hair.

"That's all we need. A bunch of crooks ready to put us at the top of their payback list."

"Sorry I got you mixed up in this," Bolan said.

"Sure you are," Riba said, a slow smile creasing his lips. "Hell, Cooper, that's what the Lone Ranger said to Tonto every time he got shot at. So what do we know about this Lise Delaware?"

"Not much. I'll ask Brognola to run a check on her." Bolan paused. "Rackham said something about her. She holds grudges. Doesn't forget. And she takes great pleasure in hurting people."

"Could make for a hell of a relationship," Riba said.

"Joshua, let's get out of here soon as Duncan shows up."

"You got it, Cooper." He took in Bolan's exhausted expression. "You don't look too good."

"Right now I don't feel it. And that's the truth."

Bolan slumped into a chair, letting the pistol slip from his fingers. The disturbing emotions inside his head were intensifying. It was as if every single thought and emotion was vying for immediate attention, each competing with the other. He could see Riba watching him, concern on his face.

Bolan was exhausted. His body ached from head to toe. He couldn't even begin to locate a spot that didn't hurt. The whole experience of the mission, from day one, blew up in his face and a heavy darkness engulfed him. Sight and sound and feeling collapsed in on him and Bolan, for once, didn't try to fight it.

Epilogue

Order as such took its own time to be restored, and those involved were part of that restoration.

With the facility and the safehouse under FBI control and the CDC monitoring the lab, immediate concerns were being met.

The FBI brought in its IT experts and they went through every computer and cell phone, digging deep and extracting information that helped to build a picture of exactly what had taken place. Even though the federal agency worked with the best personnel and equipment, building a picture of the obscure organization turned out to be a long and frustrating undertaking. After a number of weeks the organization was still beyond reach except for a few minor breakthroughs.

The exposure of the insider who had betrayed Vic Bremner was a success. After painstaking efforts an encrypted file found on a laptop from the facility was broken and a number of names exposed. Among these names was that of the agent who had been paid to provide information on anyone getting close. Money paid to the man, hidden in three separate bank accounts under false names, showed he had accepted close to a quarter of a million dollars. Presented with the facts, the agent broke down and admitted his crimes. Agent Vic Bremner was still dead.

The theft of the smallpox virus from the CDC in Atlanta wasn't discovered for a couple of weeks. Dr. Helen Tasker and her investigating team eventually discovered the theft was the work of a lab tech with a growing drug habit who had been bought off and had smuggled out a vial of the virus from the sample she was working on. The young woman had been arrested and held for trial. A week later she was found dead in her cell from a fatal overdose of a powerful narcotic. No needle was ever found. The killer wasn't identified.

Ray Callum suffered a similar fate. On his way to a safe-house he was shot through the head as he stepped from the transfer vehicle. A long search eventually located the place where the shooter had fired from. It was an extremely long shot, the slug having come from a Russian-made Dragunov sniper rifle. The shooter had been extremely accurate. As with the lab tech's killer, no one was identified. The trail ran cold.

FBI SAC Duncan began to understand what he was up against. The group behind the smallpox affair was openly challenging the federal authorities, showing they were powerful enough to defy the FBI and remove potentially dangerous witnesses at will. Duncan refused to bow down to the unseen enemy. The situation simply drew out his stubborn side, and he promised himself he wouldn't back down from apprehending the organization.

Within his department he chose a tight group of agents he knew he could rely on. They were brought directly under his jurisdiction, their task being to look into every aspect of the current investigation. Duncan knew it was going to be a long slog. That didn't worry him. He was no weekend warrior. Duncan was in it for the duration.

One small victory came his way when Lawrence Pembury's wife and child were located and rescued. Pembury was still in isolation when his family was brought to see him. Seeing them gave him a boost. Duncan took a personal interest in the matter and interceded with immigration authorities, helping to get Pembury's wife and child their documents so they could stay in the U.S.

Kim Jeung Pak, the South Korean agent—Bolan never learned his real name—was recovered enough from his wound to return home after a few weeks. Preventing the smallpox virus from being taken by the North Korean cell, on both occasions, was a satisfactory result for the agent, even though it had taken place under unexpected circumstances. The involvement of the man known only as Cooper was the main factor in that result.

WHILE TAKING WELL-DESERVED R & R at a hospice, Bolan had frequent visitors. He spent a few days in bed, his body slowly recuperating from the abuse it had received, before he was allowed to move around. Bolan had no objections to the time he spent alone, staring out through the window of his room. His body would heal in its own time.

It was the slower, frustrating healing of his mind that concerned him. As the physical trauma faded and the stressless atmosphere of his surroundings allowed him to simply regenerate his thoughts, Bolan made no demands. He simply allowed everything to wash over him.

His first visitor was Joshua Riba. The Apache had come to tell Bolan he was on his way home. Back to his New Mexico haunts. He showed Bolan the new jacket he'd purchased to replace the one that had been bullet-holed.

"Now I feel better," Riba said. "You getting there, friend?"

Bolan nodded. "Thanks for the help, Joshua."

"Was a pleasure."

"You ever need my help, just call."

"And if you want to come and take the Apache cure, the offer stands."

"I just might do that when I'm done here," Bolan said. "Is Brognola taking care of you?"

"Fixed me up with a private plane to get me home. All to myself. I need to get home before I get too used to all this luxury." Riba thrust out a big hand. "You'll have to watch your own back now I'm leaving. And keep in touch." ╴

LEO TURRIN AND BROGNOLA made a combined visit. Bolan managed to put faces and names together.

Turrin was full of apologies. He carried some guilt over what had happened to Bolan.

"Leo, none of us knows how a mission is going to go until we're in the middle of it. Nothing runs exactly to plan. Did we get the outcome we wanted?"

"Yes."

"Then we did okay."

"Except for Vic Bremner."

"He pointed the finger in Rackham's direction," Brognola said. "If he hadn't, that virus sale might have gone ahead. Hell, think of the number of dead if the North Koreans had used it."

"Any indication of the target?" Bolan asked.

"The South Korean agency is tracking the cell behind it. They believe it's a fanatic group that wants to cause unrest with the south. The North Korean government is denying any involvement."

"I'd be surprised if they didn't," Turrin said.

They spent some time on idle conversation. Bolan realized it had been advised by his doctor, a distracting way to ease his thoughts on familiar ground.

"You look tired, Striker," Brognola said. "We'll leave you to it."

DAYS LATER, SEATED IN the quiet dayroom, Bolan felt a shadow fall across his face. He looked up and recognized Laura Devon.

Only she looked altogether different.

She was in military uniform.

"Look at you, Sergeant," Bolan said.

⸍hair and sat facing him.

"You are looking better," she said. "Well, at least a *little* better."

"Ever the flatterer." Bolan examined her uniform. "No doubt about it. You make that uniform look good."

"I realized all I was doing was hiding away in Hardesty. Flipping eggs and frying bacon was just an excuse. The time I spent around you. What we went through. It told me to get off my butt and move on with my life. I was still in the reserves, so I called my old commander and said I wanted back in."

"They're lucky to have you."

"That's to be seen."

Bolan reached out and touched her cheek. "No," he said. "It's a fact. You'll be fine, Laura Devon."

"And what about you, Cooper? Are you going to be fine?"

"Doctor says the scans he took show the pressure on my brain is subsiding. Give it a few weeks and I should be okay."

"Only *should,* Cooper? Where's your optimism? I remember a guy who kept going, dragging me behind him, and who refused to quit no matter what was thrown at him. I want to remember that when I'm in the middle of a firefight and I'm ready to run for cover. Cooper, you'll come through this. I know you will."

When she kissed him before she walked away, Bolan understood.

He was alive.

He had faced his enemies and come through.

Again.

The future stretched ahead, and he would be a part of it, taking the fight to the enemy. Alive to fight another day.

* * * * *

TAKE 'EM FREE

2 action-packed novels
plus a mystery bonus

NO RISK

NO OBLIGATION
TO BUY